HOOD Symphony

A NOVEL BY AUTHOR

TNICYO

G
STREET CHRONICLES

JUN 1 2

PA

Published by:

G Street Chronicles
P.O. Box 490082
College Park, GA 30349
www.gstreetchronicles.com
fans@gstreetchronicles.com

Cover Design: Hot Book Covers
                 www.hotbookcovers.com

ISBN: 978-1-9384429-8-8
LCCN: 2012937134

Join us on our social networks
Facebook
G Street Chronicles Fan Page
G Street Chronicles "A New Urban Dynasty" Readers' Group
Twitter
@gstrtchroni

HOOD Symphony

Acknowledgements

First, To my Creator, my beginning and my end; thank you for the gift to imagine, love and live a fulfilling life.

Thanks to my mother for never placing limits on anything I could do, and always being the wind beneath my wings. You are the best—I love you.

To My husband, I wish you love, grace, and peace always.

To My baby girl, You are my sunshine and the reason I wake everyday with a smile and will. Love you, Bebe.

To My loving and fun family who are also my fabulous friends, thanks for holding me down. You're the greatest for putting up with me even when I acted like I'd lost my mind along the way; Thanks to my little brother, Casey, Love you, and know you will do big things. Keep up the good work; To Dred Dynamite, thanks for the support and management advice; To Alex B. Coe, thanks for agreeing to style me. Hollywood stylists better watch out because you are a force to be reckoned with; to Geri, Kap, Dre, and Zack, thanks for your support and enthusiasm; Thanks To Ronanaldis (the it wiz), for helping with my editing; to C-mac, Grace, Natasha, and Chris, thanks for reading the draft and giving your honest feedback; to all of my real friends, you know who you are. Thumpkin, you already know who you are in the book (wink, wink).

This book is dedicated in loving memory of a man who was indeed a ray of sunshine in everyone's life he touched...

Benjamin L. Collins

G STREET CHRONICLES
~A NEW URBAN DYNASTY~

WWW.GSTREETCHRONICLES.COM

Chapter ONE

Tiffany woke up yet another morning suffering from morning sickness and again wishing like she had for the past month, that Tree was next to her making her feel better, and giving her some of the beast. No matter how pregnant she was, it was hands down that his sex was the bomb and could cure all things. Thinking a shower might calm her, she lathered her body reminiscing how she ended up with the love of her life and living in a 1.5 million dollar mini-mansion. Tiffany had been through a lot before she met Tree and promised herself she would never go back to the old life. Tree might be the bread winner in the house but she was, for sure, the boss lady, and if things didn't go her way there was bound to be some shit. End of discussion.

Tree and Tiffany met five years earlier at a party her cousin, Diamond, dragged her to just to get her out of the house. Finals were over and all Tiffany wanted to do was relax, drink wine, and watch movies alone, but her cousin was not trying to hear all that on a Saturday night. She was still trying to cope with her breakup with Jay, and did not want to deal with the petty girls that lived in the area and always hated on her and Diamond because they always rocked the flyest and newest shit. They, on the other hand, were 'Cato's' and 'It's Fashion' queens and, even then, still could not put an outfit together to save their lives. She also was content staying in because going out probably meant running into Jay or some of his friends. She knew if someone said something to her there was sure to be some shit. She was not good at arguing, but much better at knocking a bitch out and being done with the whole situation. Regardless of her excuses, Diamond was not trying to hear it, so Tiffany decided to go to make her happy and get her off her back.

With that, Diamond was satisfied and knew Von would be very proud of her for convincing Tiffany to come out. He had for a minute, wanted to hook Tiffany up with his right hand man and, with Jay out the way, he knew it would be a match made in hood-heaven. While Tiffany showered, Diamond rolled a blunt and poured herself a glass of wine. They had recently shopped in New York, spending well over $10,000 on clothes, jewelry and shoes and were bound to be, as always, fly and fresh to the death. Smelling fresh after her shower, Tiffany sashayed back to her room pondering what to wear and how to style her hair. It was not out of the norm that her cousin had made a decision for her, had her outfit hanging outside the closet door, and was waiting to pull her hair up in a sweep style. By the time they got out of the house Tiffany was feeling good and ready to party. Diamond was successful in getting her tipsy, relaxed, and back to the way she was before the breakup.

When they pulled up in Diamond's Mercedes S500, the crowd was bananas and they were thankful that Von was cool with the bouncers and instead of standing in line, they could go straight into the VIP entrance. They valet parked, walked pass the crowd, with haters giving them the evil eye, and sashayed their happy, tipsy asses right into VIP.

Once inside, Tiffany surveyed the crowd and saw that it was jumping this Saturday, and was ready to join in and get her dance on. They passed a few of Jay's friends. Tiffany spoke and kept it moving. A couple of them tried to holler at her, but she was not trying to hear the bullshit. She knew these same lames would drop everything at the drop of a dime when Jay called them, like a bunch of bitch-ass niggas. Tiffany was about business and had no interest in anyone who didn't share her enthusiasm for making money. When they arrived at Von's table, bottles of Moet and Grey Goose were plentiful and flowing freely. Von and Tiffany hugged, then he made them a drink. As always, Diamond was playing her wife roll boo'ed up with Von. Tiff didn't care because her mind was made up—being dressed to the nine in her Jimmy Choo's and Versace kimono-style, silk, mini dress—she was going to have a good time. Out the corner of her eyes she spotted a guy standing off to the side by himself, chilling on the wall. She watched him a little while not believing how fine this man was. He was definitely eye candy. She wondered if he was local because she had never seen him before. She saw a couple of girls approach him flirting, but he didn't seem fazed, and who could blame him since most of them looked like rejects.

Diamond came over to make sure she was OK. Tiffany asked who the mystery man was, and if she had ever seen this fine, chocolate, 6'5", muscular-built, man before.

Diamond laughed and said, "Girl, that is Von's right-hand man, if you get out a little and hang with us you would know who he is. His name is Tree, he grew up in Maryland, was doing business there, but when he and Von decided to branch out, Tree headed to Atlanta to set up shop." She further filled her in that Tree was a heavy hitter and made Jay's money look like chump change.

Tiffany had no idea that this very man was the one that Jay answered to and bought major weight from. She could not believe her ears because just by visual, there were no signs he was a heavy hitter. Usually she would not have looked at a plain Joe type dude that showed no signs of balling… even though he was fine. Not that she was a gold digger, she had plenty money of her own, thanks to Jay giving her start-up money to open the restaurant of her dreams. She was smart enough, unlike most girls, to take what Jay called an allowance, make investments, and save. Tiffany was no fool. Her mother always taught her to save aggressively for a rainy day and warned her when she hooked up with Jay that he was snakish. But this man, that she could not take her eyes off, seemed to have some effect on her and she had not even spoken to him or felt his touch. He just radiated electricity through her just looking at him. Although she had vowed she was done with niggas in the life, she had to meet him. Tiffany asked her cousin to introduce them. She was not worried about him turning her down like he had done the other girls because she believed there were very few men that didn't want her. She was 5'11", caramel brown skin, hazel eyes, legs that didn't quit, an ass a man would be willing to die for and shoulder length, dark brown hair with light brown highlights. Yeah, Tiffany knew he would not turn her down.

Diamond called Tree over, introduced Tiffany as her cousin, and Tree as Von's right-hand man, who was back in town. Tree smiled, and damn if he didn't have dimples that were so deep she wanted to stick her fingers in them.

He extended his hand and told Tiffany it was his pleasure to meet her. The two stood for what seemed like forever holding hands and staring at each other, like their bodies had their own conversation going on. Yeah, they were instantly attracted to each other at first sight.

As if on cue, Von called and motioned Diamond over to him leaving the two alone.

Diamond said, "Great timing baby. I'm happy you were paying attention for once because I sure couldn't figure out how to excuse myself and leave them alone."

Von laughed and said, "Since it was his idea, and a great one at that, he had to be on his P's and Q's."

They went back to their table and rolled up to get their VIP party cracking in full swing. Their work was done and they were sure it would be a success. Diamond asked Von about the only small problem in his plan, Tree's girlfriend, Nina. He wasn't worried. Although Tree was wifing her, she was no match when it came to Tiff. Plus in recent conversations Tree expressed he was sick of Nina's jealousy, and how lazy she had become since he hooked up with her. It was true at times when Tree was on the road he kept company with other women but, in his mind, he did it because Nina was a bore and always had excuses why she couldn't travel with him. She also had a problem with giving head and letting her man get it when he wanted it. Yeah, Nina was a little problem that was basically no problem at all.

Tree and Tiffany sat at an empty booth to get acquainted. He ordered a bottle of Hypnotic, complimented Tiffany's outfit and took in her beauty. A couple of hood-rats who assumed she was still Jay's lady stopped at the booth to speak or more likely to flirt with Tree. He politely shot them down and sent them on their way. As they walked away, one loudly asked Tiffany how Jay was doing.

Instead of getting upset, she asked, "Why? Are you suffering from separation anxiety since his dick is not stuck in your mouth at the moment?"

With that the girl mean mugged her and walked away, calling her a bitch under her breath.

Tree smiled and said, "So you know Jay, huh?"

Tiffany filled him in that she and Jay had a relationship that ended because Jay had too much bitchassness in him to deal with a women who was street savvy, but far from stooping to being a hood rat at all times. Tree changed the subject, but since she had let him in on her latest relationship she thought she deserved to know if this man was taken.

"So Tree, are you married or boo'ed up with someone?"

He responded, "Something like that, but it ain't nothing that can't be snuffed if you trying to give me the time of day."

Tiffany smiled inwardly, liking how smooth he was, the fact that he was up-front and was not trying to feed her a line of bullshit. They talked over two hours getting acquainted and real cozy in the private booth. Jaheim's *Just in Case* came on and he pulled her up to dance. His touch sent chills up her spine and her thong became soaking wet. She prayed she wouldn't drip on the floor, because that would be truly embarrassing. She wasn't sure if she was horny because she had not had sex since her break up with Jay four months ago, or if it was the fact that this man rubbing against her felt like he had a damn snake in his pants. Whatever it was, she hoped the song would end soon or she might have to let go of her principles and fuck this man tonight. When the song was finally over, Tiffany silently gave thanks.

Diamond approached them ready to call it a night. Tiffany

thanked Tree for a good time and told him she would see him around. Diamond was geeked when they got in the car and wanted to know if she had gotten his number or given hers.

Tiffany laughed and said, "You know I don't call no nigga...he didn't ask for the number and I did not offer. If we see each other again cool, if not at least he entertained me and got my juices flowing."

During the ride home Tiff told her cousin about the dance and how she was sure she was going to drip on the floor. They shared a laugh as they pulled up to Tiffany's condo. Tiffany kissed her on the cheek, told her to drive home safely, and be on time tomorrow afternoon for their trip to Charlotte for the family reunion. She reminded Diamond not to get crazy and pack her whole damn closet because she did not want her 745 BMW weighted down with all her shit. Diamond waved her off and pulled out.

Chapter TWO

It was noon, and Tiffany struggled to get out of bed, wanting to sleep even longer after being out until about 5 AM. She showered and put her luggage in the truck so she would be ready to roll when Diamond arrived. She called Von's phone, after Diamond's lazy ass refused to answer hers, and told him to get his lazy ass wife up and to her house in an hour.

Von laughed and said he would have her there within the hour. He asked, "What did you think about my boy?"

She joked with him. He was like a big brother she never had, all up in her business. She said, "Dude was cool and seemed to be down to earth."

Von asked if they exchanged numbers.

She giggled, "I'm sure you already know the answers to these questions."

As soon as their conversation ended, her phone rang. Without looking at the caller ID, she answered "Von, what do you want?"

The voice on other end however, was not Von but Jay. When she realized who it was, she snapped and asked, "Why the fuck are you calling my phone?"

"WOW! Why you got to talk to your man like that? I was just calling to see how you were doing. You know I still love you even though you refused to forgive me for fucking that chick. You was acting like I ain't take care of home, and I ain't love you. You know the streets, you know how it gets at times."

The more he spoke, the more she wished he was near so she could slap the shit out him and punch his ass in the mouth. He really knew how to push her buttons but, unlike when they were a couple, this argument was not going to end up in some straight buck-wild fucking to make it all better. No. This would end up with both of them in lockup. She was going to end this call right now.

"Look Jay, I'm not really sure why you called, but lose my fucking number. I'm sure your little groupies told you they saw me at the club last night, but tell your girlie crew to mind theirs and let me do me."

Jay sighed loudly, "You are always so full of yourself… that's why I will always love you. I called because I know you're on your way to Charlotte for your family reunion. I wanted to get up with you, maybe do some shopping, dinner or something, as old friends."

Irritated to no end Tiffany shrilled, "I don't think so," and hung up.

Tiffany heard Von's car pull up, grabbed her bags and keys and headed out the door. Heading down 95 South, she told her cousin about the call from Jay. Diamond silently responded by pulling out a blunt and sipping her drink. Tiffany knew then she would be the designated driver the entire trip. Loud music nearly drowned out the ringing phone from an unknown number. She noticed the blinking light, hit ignore and continued cruising with Mary J. Mary J always got her down the road with no problems. The phone rang again from the same number. She wondered why people won't get the hint, and leave a message. This time though the caller did leave a message and she was anxious to know who the unknown caller was. She speed-dialed voicemail and damn near ran off the road from the sound of the deep melodious voice.

Diamond sat up and asked, "What the fuck is the problem?"

Tiffany was ecstatic she had just gotten a message from Tree.

Diamond smiled and asked, "Can we live long enough for you to at least see if he is worth getting all wet on the dance floor for, please?"

Tiffany thought about the call for a minute and questioned, "Wait a minute bitch, how did he get my number if I didn't give it to him?"

Diamond played dumb and asked, "How am I supposed to know? I'm with you."

Tiffany knew then she had been set up by Diamond and Von, but deep down, she was happy that he was pursuing her. She decided to wait a couple of days before calling him back because a girl was suppose to make him chase her, not be so pathetic and end the chase on the first call. Yeah, she would make him wonder. She was sure he was used to getting his way, so he had to learn the rules of the boss lady's handbook. Things were her way or the highway. That was her new motto since breaking up with Jay. She didn't mind loving a man and giving her heart, but she was damn if he was going to be in full control. Nope! The boss was in the driver's seat. She smiled at the possibility and continued cruising down

95. They arrived in Charlotte about seven hours later, and Jay had been blowing her phone up most of the way. She was tempted to turn the shit off, but knew as the family arrived in town they would be calling to hook up, especially her cousins from Atlanta. They had already let it be known that they were going to hit the clubs to make this year's reunion big fun. After getting settled and stuffing her face, Tiff checked her messages and had two more from Tree, and six from bitch-ass Jay. She was relaxing on the couch until the door bell rang. No one made an effort to answer it. She opened the door, assuming it was family, and to her surprise Jay was standing at her grandmother's door. He had the gall? She stepped outside and lost it.

"Why the fuck do you feel the need to play yourself by coming here? Didn't I tell you we had nothing to discuss and we sure as hell have no need to see each other."

"Damn baby, chill. I was just in the neighborhood and since you're acting like we can't be friends, I figured I would stop by anyway to make sure you're OK, and to holler at some of your family that I was cool with."

Tiffany laughed in his face and asked, "Are you finished playing yourself?

Jay, trying to act devastated said, "Look, Tiffany, enough of your drama. I fucked up and I'm sorry. Now you need to grow up and think at least on the good times. Shit was not always bad Tiff. You were my first love and I still love you."

Diamond came to the door, spoke cordially to Jay and asked him to excuse them for a minute while she spoke to her cousin. Taking Tiffany aside, she whispered, "Look here bitch, you call yourself the boss lady, now act like one. Instead of acting a fool and letting this nigga get to you, act like you're suppose to. If he wants to take you shopping, then bitch shop till your feet bleed and make sure he doesn't leave the mall till his pockets are empty. Then have a nice dinner and come home so we can party. Oh…and make sure you pick me up a couple of things because a bitch has to be compensated for her advice. OK, Tiff, you're dismissed." With that, Diamond walked away and did not think twice about looking to see if Tiffany was still standing in the same spot because she knew her cousin well enough to know she would take her advice and do as told.

Chapter THREE

After Tiffany was sure she had bled his pockets damn near dry, she told him she needed to get back to her grandmother's and get ready to hang with her cousins since they had been blowing her phone up. She really was ready to get away from Jay because it was reminding her too much of the old days when it was good between them, and she was riding with him no matter what, but he wanted to make one more stop. She told him she would wait on the bench while he did his errand. He slipped off to Tiffany's which was her favorite store since they shared the same name.

Jay was furious when he found out that Tiffany was at the club hugged up with that nigga, Tree. He was not going to let him have her even if he was married. Shit, Tiffany didn't know he was married. No. Jay was going to get her mind blown back on him. Damn if he was going to let Tree shine on him. It was bad enough the nigga was making him look like he was on McDonald's payroll and Tree was the owner. He had enough. He was not going to have Tiffany too. In Tiffany's he decided on a platinum, pear-shaped, 5carat diamond ring.

Yeah, he was going to propose to her, even though he had no intentions of marrying her, since he was already married. She was accustomed to being showered with material things and it always seemed to get him out of hot water with her. He walked back to Tiffany on the bench, thinking this bitch is so materialistic with all those bags around her, happy as shit. Little does she know that is chump change. Fuck Tiffany's happiness. He was just making sure that she felt what it was really like to not have him, and to make sure she was not going to ball out with that nigga, Tree. He would just string her along long enough for Tree to move on to the next.

When she stood up to leave, he dropped to his knees, remembering all the times she bitched about why she was good enough to shack up with but not good enough to marry. Jay looked up to her, put on his best game, and asked Tiffany to marry him. She was truly shocked at the proposal and even more shocked at the size of the diamond. So many thoughts were running through her head, she was not sure what to say. She had loved and had been faithful to this man for three years. Without giving it much thought she said, "Yes."

He slipped the ring on her finger, grabbed and kissed her deep and passionately just like old times. To his surprise, he too was feeling the way he had before shit went sour between them. He pulled out an envelope containing $5,000, told her he had a lot of stuff to take care of on the street, and would get with her after her night out with her cousins. He told her he would swing by and get them a suite at the Westin so they could celebrate their new engagement. Elated with the proposal and ring, she agreed and he dropped her off at her grandmother's.

Before she got out the car she begged him to put off business till tomorrow and just be hers tonight. He kissed her again and said, "I have to collect tonight before them street niggas get slick and try to shit me, and I'll have to add a body to the streets."

She knew by the look on his face that he was not being entirely truthful. One thing she was always able to tell was when Jay lied. Just like the many times she had asked about his cheating, she knew when he lied but she chose to shake it off up until the night she caught him in her truck fucking the shit out of a bitch in the back seat. Seeing that was the last straw for her. No. Tiffany knew this nigga was lying and she was not going to be the fool this go-round. She put on her best smile and told him she looked forward to seeing him later at the suite. Tiffany surveyed the yard to see which of her cousins were outside and spotted the one she was looking for, Diamond. She got out of Jay's Hummer, waving as he slowly pulled off. She told her cousin Poochie to give her keys to his Range Rover and without question, he did. She knew Jay didn't know Poochie's car.

Diamond knew what was up, didn't ask questions, just climbed in the passenger seat and rode out. As they followed Jay, it was clear that he was not headed near the hood to collect money. No, he was headed toward the Ballantyne area where all the ballers live with their trophy wives, but go elsewhere to play. Jay was headed someplace he had forgotten to mention to his new fiancé. As he pulled up to a plush three level home, situated on 2 acres of land, Tiffany fell back and watched as he used a garage door opener to open the door. She was wondering how stupid could she be to have missed the fucking opener on the visor. Diamond sat quiet and watched.

When he pulled into the garage, before he had the chance to lower the door a woman greeted him with a hug, and handed him a young baby, about two months old.

Tiffany couldn't contain herself. She jumped out of the truck on a mission, her cousin on her heels, still never saying a word. They stepped into the garage while Jay's back was still turned, startling the woman. She tapped him on the shoulder, he turned and damn near dropped the baby.

Jay started to stutter trying to come up with a quick lie. "Tiffany, now you're into following me. Baby, what's up? I just came through to see how Shay was doing."

Tiffany smirked, but Shay knew all to well what that smirk meant. Shit was about to hit the fan, and hard.

Shay and Tiffany were friends in Maryland. At least she pretended to be while being envious of her for all the things Jay laced her with. Shay and Jay started fucking around about two years ago behind Tiffany's back. The funny thing was Jay was cheating on Shay too because she was not the girl she had caught him fucking in her car. Diamond eyed Shay and shook her head because she had warned her cousin about that trick a while back. There was something about her Diamond never liked and now she knew why. The bitch was a snake. Jay lied that he had run into Shay a couple months after he moved to Charlotte. She was pregnant, had no place to live, her baby-daddy had kicked her out, told her he was done with her ass and said the baby was not his. On the strength of her being Tiffany's friend, he let her and her baby live in his basement.

The more he talked, the worse it got for him. He handed Shay the baby and tried to hug Tiffany which was the wrong move on his part. Before he knew it, Tiffany had spit a razor from her mouth and cut him straight across the arm. His natural reaction was to swing on her, but being the bitch he was he missed as she ducked and Diamond caught his ass in the jaw. Shay tried to run into the house but Diamond knew shit would get ugly fast and she was out of her territory. She pulled her piece and warned both of them to be the still. They were fucking up her buzz and the one thing she could not stand was a sober motherfucker messing up her buzz because they were hating. Yes, Diamond felt it best everyone be still till she got her mind right. Jay could not believe his luck. How could he have a gun pulled on his ass in his own house by a bitch and he was unarmed? Shay began to cry but no one, especially Tiffany, cared about her crying…she wanted blood. Always fast with her hands, she walked up to Shay and punched her so hard she fell back. A diva yes, but always a street bitch first. She caught Shay and prevented her from hitting the floor because she knew the baby didn't deserve to be harmed. When she got a good look at the baby, she realized he looked just like Jay. She wanted to cry because he had always told her that once they stacked their money they would start a family, and the whole while he had started one with a bitch that called herself Tiffany's friend.

Jay had enough and told them to get the fuck off his property. He told Tiffany to suck the shit up and don't be mad that she was not women enough for him, so he had to go to Shay. He blabbered he never intended to have any babies with her ass because she was not worthy. If so, she wouldn't have miscarried what was to be his first born.

He laughed at her saying, "No one is going to want you when they realize your insides are all fucked up and probably rotten. No, I got me a real woman, one that could hold and keep a baby for me, ain't always wanting to go shopping and she works and shit, and is willing to take care of her man."

Tiffany was hurt…hurt because he knew how depressed and upset she had been when she lost her baby five months into her pregnancy. Shay pretended to be there for her as a home girl, but she guessed now that is when the bitch decided to plot and give him the one thing Tiffany had not given him so far. Diamond was so furious she turned her burner around and hit Jay in the head, instantly taking the smile off his face. Shay put the baby down and was trying to come to her man's defense.

Diamond warned her, "I never liked you, so your best bet would be to fall back because I have no problem bagging your ass."

Tiffany backed up because her heart couldn't take anymore. On her way out the garage she stopped at Jay's truck and took both of his pistols. She thought to herself, some habits never die. Diamond got in the driver seat and drove back to their grandmother's house.

Chapter FOUR

On the ride back Tiffany's phone rang but she really was not in the mood to talk. Her cousin was on the phone with Von reenacting the events that had just taken place. Without looking at the caller ID she answered the phone, but didn't speak, just listened. To her surprise it was Tree and his voice immediately soothed her. He spoke again and this time Tiffany responded, unable to play any games with him.

"Hi Tree, how are you?"

"So you know a nigga voice, huh?"

"I've been meaning to call you back but it seems as though my life went from bad to worse."

"Well what's up ma…why you sounding like someone died?"

Tiffany was too tired and hurt to even bullshit, so she told him everything that happened. He listened to her chain of events as he puffed on a blunt. When she finished, she broke down and cried. Diamond was somewhat shocked that her cousin confided in someone other than her and, of all people, Tree. But she knew Tree was a good man and he would never hold shit over her cousin's head. When Tiffany finished spilling her guts to Tree, he calmly asked where she was.

She said, "In Charlotte, for a family reunion."

He laughed and said, "Yeah, ma, I got that much. I've done my homework. What I mean is where in Charlotte?"

"We're riding around uptown." She thought Diamond was riding around giving her time to get herself together before heading back to face the family.

Tree said, "OK. You're uptown, cool. Tell Diamond to drop you off. She knows what's up."

"I beg your pardon!"

Without answering or explanation, he hung up. Tiffany looked at her cousin for an answer, repeating what Tree said, and asked, "What the hell is going on? I am not getting on the highway at this time of the night. I ain't up for no late night runs. Let's just go back to Nanna's and call it a fucking night."

Diamond pulled up to entrance of the Ritz Carlton. Before Tiffany could ask why, the passenger door opened, scaring the shit out of her and of all people, Tree was standing there.

"What's up Diamond, nice to see you."

"It's Nice to see you, Tree."

He took her hand and removed the ring. She started to object, but had no energy to argue with another soul. He helped her out of the truck, shut the door, and waved goodbye to Diamond. They walked into the lobby holding hands, but not conversing. They stopped at the registration desk to make friendly conversation with a clerk Tree noticed at check-in. They talked mostly about her employment with the hotel for two years to pay for college tuition, majoring in bio-chemistry. Tree wished her luck and said, "Here's a little something to help with the bills, but before anything else, get an appraisal. Being a bio-chemist major means you ain't no fool, so don't fuck up."

The clerk was dumbfounded and looked from him to Tiffany. Tiffany too was confused. He rattled on about someone giving his girl a gift to try to win her over. "Being that she don't need for nothing, she surely don't need gifts from a thug. I saw you earlier deep in your books and could see you're no hoochie. I wanted to give this to someone who would make good use of it."

The clerk looked at the ring and quickly handed it back explaining they were not allowed to accept gifts from guests. When Tiffany saw how big Tree's heart was, she opened up and said, "What they don't know will not kill them. Take it. The value is 25K and it should appraise for not less than 20K."

After she graciously accepted with their word that this would be just between the three of them, Tree took Tiffany's hand and headed to the elevator.

Tiffany was exhausted and anxious to forget the events of the day. When they reached their floor, Tree picked her up and carried her to their room, putting her down in the bathroom doorway. Candles were the only light in the room with a garden tub filled with bubbles and floating rose petals. On the vanity was a fluffy pink robe, slippers and a tee. Tree pulled her further into the bathroom, walked out and closed the door. She undressed, got in the tub, and cried like she had never cried before. How could she be a fool for the same nigga twice and she called herself the boss. Shit, she should fire herself for the dumb shit she had subjected herself to.

While Tiffany was relaxing in the tub, Tree called Von and assured him he would take good care of Tiffany, and needed him to do a favor and contact a couple of people. Tree lit another blunt and waited for Von to call back. He would not act right now on Jay. No, he would let the smoke clear on his ass and make him believe there was no bad blood. He already knew Tiffany and Diamond had given the nigga a run for his money, so it would not look good if anything happened to him right now. He would wait. But he would make his ass pay for trying to get at him through her. If it was one thing he could not stand it was a hating-ass nigga that just refused to know his place. Von called 15 minutes later saying that everything was set up, he passed the message, and told him to expect a call in about 5 minutes.

Tree had just made drinks when Tiffany came out of the bathroom, her hair pulled up into a ponytail, wearing just the tee and thongs. She walked over to the window, viewing the uptown skyline, wishing she was home in her bed, and over the depression that she has been going through for months. Not wanting to crowd her, Tree sat back in his chair and observed her.

After several minutes of silence, she asked, "When, how, and why are you in Charlotte?"

He smiled, something she swore she could get use to, and said, "You would not return my calls so I came down to see what the problem was."

She thought, OK, either he is crazy as hell or he is really into me. Either way it was a nice gesture. She sat on the sofa next to him, looking stern, and asked, "What exactly do you expect from me? If it's a game, I'm not in the mood to play and if it's sex, you can forget it."

"Sex? That's comical. You're funny, Ma. I'm going to fly all the way down here for sex when there are girls lined up, if only to smell my dick, and I'm flying to one for sex. Naw!

To be real with you, I dug the vibe and conversation we had at the club, and it didn't hurt that you're fine as hell. So I figured I can't get you to call to get to know you better, so I would just come to you. Then when I heard the shit you hit me with, it's a good thing I came."

She suddenly felt embarrassed for having told Tree, a stranger, how she had gotten played by another nigga. Now what was to stop him from doing the same thing to her if she was to even get with him at that level? Well that settled that...there was nothing happening with them no matter how fine he was.

He sensed her discomfort and moved closer to her, lifted her head with his hand, looked into her eyes and said, "No matter what the nigga before me did, I ain't him. There is a difference between a man and a boy, an employer and employee."

Like her, he considered himself a boss, but her actions today were far from boss material.

She was tired and excused herself to rest for a few.

"Help yourself and if you need me, I'll be right here, chilling."

She got up to leave and hoped she would not regret what she was about to ask. "Tree, will you come and lay with me until I fall asleep? Right now I just need to be next to you."

Without another word, he got up and followed her to the bedroom. Her heart in her stomach; she couldn't shake how Shay and Jay played her. She thought they both deserved much more then what she gave them but, more than anything, she just couldn't wait to get out of Charlotte and back home. She longed to be back to her life of restaurateur and devoting her energy to her business. Tree empathized with her gloom knowing she would not sleep with thoughts of that nigga nagging her. As calm as he usually was, he was annoyed that he would have to wait to teach this nigga a lesson for fucking with him, and for defiantly fucking with her. He had had enough.

He pulled her close to him and could feel the tension, but she didn't put up a fight. He lifted her on him and kissed her like his life depended on it. She lost sight of everything as the kiss set off a feeling that she knew his touch from somewhere, but knew she had never met him before. His kiss felt as if he was trying to tell her his intentions without words, and she responded as if she understood and felt the same way. He removed his shirt and her tee, continuing to kiss her slowly. With their tongues intertwining, he caressed her breast. The feeling of her skin was like pure silk against his hands. He lowered his mouth to her breast taking each one into his mouth, one at a time, and sucked them as if they were pieces of ice.

Tiffany couldn't remember ever feeling like this, not even when she was with Jay. He slowly removed her thong, kissed her thighs, and ran his tongue back to her breast. The feeling of all of this was driving her wild with desire. He stopped briefly to remove his pants, and seeing him butt naked confirmed her first impression during their first dance that he had a snake in his pants. He looked at her naked body and knew he was going to keep her for his. Tree started slowly at her feet, placing one toe at a time in his mouth and sucking each one. She had never experienced anything like it, but had heard her girls talk about their man sucking toes. This was her first pleasure of experiencing it and it was well worth the wait. As he made his way up her leg he used his fingers to part her lips, softly brushed his fingers across her clit that was now swollen. She made the decision then to lose her mind and dignity and let him have his way with her. He was so skilled with his tongue, flickering her clit and sliding his fingers in and out of her pussy. She wondered where he had been all her sexual life. Tree wanted to make sure she came twice before he could even think about entering her with his dick. He stuck his tongue in her vagina and that pretty much sealed the deal. Tiffany came so hard she thought she had pissed on herself.

He was somewhat satisfied and made sure he got every drop of it with his tongue. By now she was begging him to enter her so she could feel him inside her. He was rock hard and felt he might need to go back down on her so he could jack off to get that first nut on his own. Based just on her taste he knew if he entered her now he would come instantly. Nope, she would have to continue to beg because he was not going out like that. He kissed her, rubbed the head of his dick around the opening and clit, and flipped her over to lick down her back, causing goose bumps in anticipation. As he got closer he started to finger her pussy with two fingers while jacking his dick with his other hand. The feeling of her insides with his hand started to drive him crazy and he picked up the pace both fingering her and jacking his dick, and just as he was about to nut he felt her cum yet again as it ran down his fingers.

Satisfied, he turned her over and slowly entered her warmth, stopping just to marinate in it. As he began to move it was as if their bodies were speaking to each other and moved in synch. Tree lifted her onto him and she wrapped her legs around his waist and stared into his eyes. They made love for a good hour, until he asked her to cum for him one more time. She agreed, they kissed passionately, and came together. Tired and unable to move Tiffany relaxed as Tree cleaned her up. They spent the rest of the night wrapped in each others arms.

Tiffany woke to the sound of her blackberry going off. She reached over and saw that it was her cousin.

"Hello."

"Girl get your ass up and get dressed, we have to go to this shit with the family. I covered for you last night I ain't doing it today."

Tiffany laughed and said, "I'll be ready in an hour."

Diamond said, "An hour! It's 12 o'clock in the afternoon, and your ass is still in bed? What really happened up in the Ritz last night?"

As her cousin continued to run her mouth, Tree rolled over and decided to make her his brunch since they had missed breakfast, and it was now lunchtime. Tree began kissing her on the neck, and made his way to her breast pushing them together so he could suck both nipples at the same time. He was addicted, but damn sure was not going to let anyone know. He had let his guard down and broke his number one rule, to run up in nothing without a condom, and because of that he had experienced with Tiffany something he had never experienced with another woman. Sure he had finger fucked enough women to know what their insides felt like with his hand, but his dick never had the pleasure of the raw deal till last night, and it felt like a piece of heaven on earth.

Tiffany felt him enter her and hung up on Diamond without even saying bye. She was sore as hell from his 10 inches all up and through her last night. And, yes, he was much bigger than Jay. But it was not just the length, he was able to work the dick and the tongue so, yeah, he was a keeper. Tiffany lost all thoughts when he kept hitting her G spot. Satisfied that he felt her cumming down his dick, he went ahead and busted a nut and was ready to start his day.

After Diamond picked Tiffany up, she instantly knew her cousin had had her world rocked and was happy for her. She decided she would wait for her to disclose the details when she was ready, and it didn't take long. Tiffany told her she was now part of the toe-sucked club. Diamond burst out laughing and congratulated her cousin.

As they were talking Tiffany's phone rang. She smiled at the name that popped up.

"Hello."

"Hey Ma, what's going on?"

"Nothing, we are just getting to my grandmother's for the festivities. What are you doing?"

" Just finished making some calls and had you on the brain, so I figured I would call. Are you coming back to spend the night with me again?"

She smiled, just thinking about it and said, "Yeah, I'll call you when I'm on my way."

"OK! That's what's up. I don't fly out till tomorrow morning at 7:00, and I want to spend as much time with you as possible. When are you coming back to Maryland?"

"I'll be leaving tomorrow too but just not as early as you."

"OK, cool. So that means I will not miss a day seeing you."

She smiled and said, "No, I guess not."

"OK. Have fun with the family and remember to hit me up."

With that he ended the call. Tiffany thought that is one thing we are going to have to work on, that hanging up shit without saying goodbye.

Ironically, Tree got a call from Jay needing a re-up. Tree

thought little did this nigga know that he was right in his town and getting ready to rock his world. He asked how much he needed and when he needed it, and told him it would be ready and, just as always, have his money, then ended the call. He then called Von to let him know what was up. Von was prepared to take care of it. Tree called to check on his mother and sister to make sure they were OK. He decided to take a nap because he was tired after last night's festivities. Five hours later he got a message on his Blackberry that Jay was supplied and money was collected. He thought to himself how dumb some niggas can be especially niggas that had no business in the game.

After he finished puffing a blunt he decided to treat himself to a shopping spree to kill some time. He called the valet to have his rental pulled around front and headed to South Park mall, grabbing a bite to eat on the way. His Blackberry went off with a message from Tiffany saying she was thinking about him. He smiled and knew then he needed to make it back to Maryland fast to take care of one last thing before she got back...Nina. Yeah, she knew Nina existed and was his girl but he wanted to change a few things and wife Tiffany instead. Plus, what Nina didn't know is he had bought a 5 acre lot that was under contract to have a mini mansion built on it and he had no intentions of moving her into it. This was a home he intended to share with Tiffany and if things went well, with their first born. Von had already told him about Tiffany's miscarriage and how depressed she had been about it. He was not sure if she remembered telling him how Jay belittled her by saying she was rotten on the inside and unable to even carry his child. Tree knew that shit happen for a reason, and she would be the mother of his first born.

Chapter FIVE

Tree called his townhouse and like clockwork, lazy-ass Nina was at the crib chilling. He asked what she was doing and she said just sitting around with her girls drinking margaritas, after they had just come in from shopping. He shook his head in disgust and hoped she enjoyed her last shopping trip on him, both her and her girls. She said she missed him and asked when he was coming home, because she needed more money if he was going to be gone longer than planned.

"Yeah? Are you missing me or missing my pockets?"

She laughed, "What type of question is that? Is there money on the street you need me to pick up?"

He frowned, and arched his brows at her question, thinking she was sounding like she had a habit or something. He had given her $20,000 before he left. How the hell she went through that money in two days was beyond him. He simply told her, "No."

Von had picked up any money that was hanging and he didn't need her to do anything but be home when he got there in the morning.

"OOHHHH, Tree are you missing me already after two days?"

"Yeah, if you want to believe that, Nina. Just be there when I get there and get them trifling bitches out of my house now!"

With that, he ended the call leaving her to talk to the tone. He called Von and asked if he had heard any rumors of anyone serving Nina on the streets because something was not sitting well with him. Von said he had not but he would keep his ears to the streets. This time Von ended the call but Tree was not fazed because that is how they did things.

Shit was getting a little too weird for Tree and he vowed that once he got Nina out of his house he was definitely be taking a trip to someone's island. Fuck the bullshit. He and Von had been in the game a long time and he still questioned the fact that both of them were worth about $200 mill, but still risking their lives on the street instead of giving the shit up. He was making a mental note to get to know Tiffany and find out her long term goals. He was ready to get the hell out of Maryland and the hell out the north period. While in the south, handling the southern connection, he had grown to like it and was giving thought to building and retiring there and hopefully, drilling a hole in Von's head to do the same.

Nina hung up the phone disgusted and wanted to slap Tree's ass. How was he just going to dismiss her like she was a nobody and he was a fucking king or something? The only reason she put up with his shit was for his money and for the love of Jay. Tree and Von had made it pretty much impossible for Jay to come up in Maryland like them. They had everything on lock which was the reason he moved to Charlotte—to establish his name and get things popping. He hoped to get there and become king when she left Tree's ass high and dry for good. Nina had been taking Tree's money for a while to help Jay get on his feet. Little did Tree's stupid ass know that the money he was charging Jay was not hurting him because, in reality, it was Tree's money, Jay was just giving him his shit back. Tree always thought he was smarter than Jay, but now the joke was on him. Nina went back to drinking with her girls totally ignoring what Tree had said because hell, he was not there like always. The reason she started fucking Jay was because Tree was usually not around to fulfill her needs. So what he wasn't doing in the bedroom, she found someone who would. Jay was not as great in bed as Tree but, hell, he got her where she needed to be. Plus, he talked to her and not at her. Since Jay was on her mind, she called him because he was due in town today, and wanted to make sure she was looking good for him when he arrived.

"Hey you, it's me, are you in town yet?"

"No, not yet. Are you coming here first?"

"Yeah, I need to get that money off you and do the pickup, then I'll be back through so you can show your daddy just how much you missed him."

Nina was satisfied and said she couldn't wait.

"Yo, you know my dogs saw your man hugged up with my old trick, Tiffany, right?"

Nina laughed. She wasn't prepared for that news. "They must be mistaken because he's out of town. I told you that."

"Yeah, I know this happened before he left a couple of weeks ago." Nina was vexed. How dare he and, of all people, that bitch. She was always walking around like she was somebody special. Nina hated her. First Jay now Tree. But she was not worried because she was wifey and no one was taking her spot till she gave it to them, and when she left he would be broke anyway.

"Well if she wants him she can have him. He ain't doing nothing for me, not like you Daddy. Plus he's about to be broke anyway and her greedy ass ain't gonna want him."

Jay laughed. "You know what baby, you are so right. But yo, I will hit you when I touch down."

Chapter SIX

Shay was getting a little sick of the bullshit, but tried to play her roll. But damn, if Jay was not fucking Tiffany, it was Nina, and she was behind both of them as the big damn secret. In addition, now he's booing Nina up on the phone with her sitting right there and she's just suppose to shut up and be quiet. Yeah, that was getting old fast and she was starting to question her decision to be with his grimy-ass, especially since she knew why Tiffany broke up with him. He was cheating on both of them. When Tiffany cried to her about finding him fucking another bitch in her truck, she wanted to cry too because he promised to stop fucking Tiffany and it would be just her. That went out the window, or better said, never happened, and still she stuck with him. Hell, after all that, Tiffany still got a bigger fucking diamond than she did, and it was just suppose to be something to keep her from getting with Tree while he collected all that money from Nina, by keeping her and Tree together.

When they arrived in Maryland, Jay asked Shay if she wanted to go to her mother's or check into a hotel. Shay preferred checking into a hotel because she suddenly felt a headache coming on. Jay checked them in and figured he better dick her down one good time before he left because he could tell she was not happy with him. He did love her because she rode with him through it all and never once said a word. He walked up behind her, pulled her head back a little to rest on his shoulder, and kissed her neck with her back against his chest. He massaged her breast and she let out a soft moan. Jay's dick began to get rock hard, but he wanted to take his time with her so it did not seem like he was just fucking her and running out the door. Jay unbuttoned her pants, slid them down, and she stepped out of them. He began to massage her clit through her silk boy shorts and felt her getting wet. He got down on his knees, pulled her shorts off and parted her legs slightly. Shay was feeling real good, until his phone rang and she knew her party was over. To her surprise, she felt him slide his finger in her and she began to tremble with Jay in between her legs. Still standing, he started to lick her clit softly and then circle around her opening. The feeling was so good to Shay she threw her head back, and tried to hold her balance and not let her legs buckle under her. Jay slid his tongue in and out of her while switching up with his fingers. Shay began to grind on his tongue because the rhythm was so good to her. She knew it was only a matter of time before she would cum. Jay was loving the taste of her juices especially since he knew that the pussy was all his and he was not sharing with anyone else. He was her second sexual partner and he intended to make sure he was her last. The rhythm was too much for her, she came all over his face and almost collapsed to the floor. Satisfied with his work, Jay got off the floor, undressed and bent her over the desk. He decided to give her breast some action so he picked her up, placed her on the desk, and took off her shirt. He kissed her, letting their tongues dance in each others mouth as he held her breast in his hands. He licked her nipples softly, taking them between his lips and nibbled on them firm but not too hard. Shay was now pulling at him to give her the dick and by now his dick was so hard it was standing at attention. He pulled her down a little closer to the edge of the desk and down on his dick. She let out a soft gasp and tightened her muscles around his dick as he slid in and out of her wetness. She let her muscles tighten and then loosen on his dick because she knew that drove him crazy. He decided to drive her crazy too and while digging in and out of her, he brought one nipple at a time to his mouth and sucked on them like he was sure something was going to come out of them.

Shay could not take it anymore and Jay didn't know how much longer he would be able to stand it before he busted. He looked into her eyes and without a word they both came at the same time. Shay fell forward collapsing onto his chest and he held onto her unable to move because his dick was still throbbing.

Chapter SEVEN

Nina was getting everything set up for Jay when he got there. She was so excited she felt like a child at Christmas. Had she known that Tree had made a call for one of his workers to watch his house and her to see what was really going on, she would have thought twice about playing with her life by having Jay in his house. Three hours after Jay touched down in Maryland, he was at Tree and Nina's door. Nina opened the door and out in broad daylight greeted him with a kiss that was sure to have them both needing oxygen. Jay lifted her up and carried her into the house. Life for Nina was about to go from sugar to shit real fast.

Ish could not believe his eyes. This bitch was bold as hell to cross Tree in his own house. Ish thought it best to call Von before calling Tree. "Yo Von, this Ish. I'm over here at this nigga Tree house doing the lookout like he asked me. Peep this, guess who just pulled up and greeted Tree's girl by sticking his tongue down her throat before carrying her off into Tree's house?"

When Ish dropped Jay's name in Von's lap, Von instructed

him to stay put, keep an eye on the house, but not to call Tree till he heard back from him. He was trying to figure out if he was to let the original plan he and Tree came up with play out, or handle this shit now and be done. Fuck it. This nigga gonna have to decide. Von picked up the phone and called Tree to deliver the news. Tree was laid up chilling with Tiffany, talking and getting to know her when he got the call. He asked Von to repeat himself, and he did. Tree knew then where his money was going. No, the bitch ain't have a habit, she had another man. Fine by Tree, but don't steal from him to give to the enemy. That was a sin. Tree told Von he would handle it and not to move. Tell Ish he can leave. He looked at Tiffany and wondered if he had the energy to put into another female.

She could tell something was wrong and asked, "What's wrong?"

He was quiet for a long time, but told her what was up.

"They don't call me boss lady for nothing, I got you."

Tiffany jumped on the phone and asked Diamond to come to the hotel. Tree was very confused as to what she was doing and found nothing funny. Tiffany changed into a business suit and Manolo Blahnik shoes. He could not help but ask what she was doing.

She said, "Old habits die hard, and we're going to get this money."

She kissed him and said if he never trusted anyone, trust her now. She knew he wasn't beat for money, but it was the principle. She kissed him again and left when Diamond arrived. Diamond was suited and blinged up, being true to her name.

When they arrived at Jay's house Tiffany jumped out, peeked through the garage window confirming no one was there, went up to the garage keypad, punched in a number, and it worked on the first try. Jay was such an ass, he never changed anything. No wonder he could never get on Von and Tree's level. Once inside the garage, she picked the door lock, something she had been good at since grammar school. Why she chose to learn lock picking, who knows, but it sure came in handy at times like this. In the house, Tiffany looked around and was not impressed at all. She figured as much time as Shay spent around her she would have learned something about decorating. Tiffany walked through the whole house, noticing that the only room with hardwoods was the living room. Damn shame…as big as the house was, they covered the floors with carpet instead of wood. She moved the couch and sure enough, like everything else he never changed, there were loose boards. They lifted the boards and found a built-in floor safe.

Tiffany said, "If his combination is the same as back in the day, when I see him again I'm going to slap him for being stupid."

She tried it, and what do you know. Her cousin laughed and said, "Guess you owe him a slapping!"

They took the money out the safe which looked like close to a mill, closed the safe and moved the couch back. Making sure everything was back the way the found it, they left the house. They both wore gloves so neither was worried about finger prints. Tiffany kissed her cousin on the cheek and thanked her for helping.

Diamond said, "Anything for you, you know that. Tree's my dude, so you know I got him."

They headed back to the hotel. Once there Tiffany jumped out of the car and entered the hotel room with a big smile. She handed Tree the bags and sat back to watch his reaction.

Tree couldn't stop staring and smiling at Tiffany, knowing what she did for him without being asked. He also thought about how hood she really was and wondered why Von had forgotten to mention that to him. He made a mental note to get with Von about that later. Tree didn't even count the money. Instead he hugged her so tight she told him she couldn't breath. He already knew he was going to make sure the money went into her account because she had worked for it and it was due her.

"Have you lost your mind taking a chance like that," he asked.

"No, I have,'t lost my mind, but he was not going to play you too. His playing card has been revoked!"

Tree laughed and said, "If only you knew. Looks like you got this cat for what looks like all his money, which was a sin because any player knows you never leave all the money you have stashed in one spot. He re-upped this morning with my fucking money. I have word on the street for no one to buy from him, so he's about to be hurting, and bad."

Tree told Tiffany his plans for Nina. She said, "If you need back-up you know I got you."

Within 24-hours they had become like a hood Bonnie and Clyde. Tiffany was trying her best not to fall for him but she was losing the battle and fast. Tree already knew from the gate she was wife material, so he was fine with the way they had been progressing, and he was even more sure about them after the job she had just pulled off, robbing Jay blind. He told her about the house he was building and asked if she ever thought about moving south.

It sounded good to her but then what about her business and her cousin? They were each others life-line. No, she could never leave her. The business, however, could always be started up again with no problems. "I could see myself moving but I would be scared of leaving everything I know and starting over."

He understood her and figured he would leave it alone for now. It was still early in their relationship. They spent the rest of the night drinking, smoking and of course, fucking in between. He just could not get enough of her and although he knew he would see her again when they got back to Maryland, he was trying to imprint her into his body.

Chapter EIGHT

After Tree got off the flight to Maryland, he was on a mission to get Nina out of his crib. He tried to think only of his good time with Tiffany and all the good things he had planned for them in the future. With those thoughts he was sure that they would keep him from killing Nina for all the shit she pulled behind his back. He had taken her from the projects, away from a mother who whipped her ass on a regular and a father who was always too drunk to protect her even if he tried. He sat in the driveway staring at his house and decided that it was time to just get the shit over with. From the rearview mirror he saw Ish and the crew pull up. He got out of the car and headed towards the house.

Nina was sitting on the couch sipping a drink and reminiscing of her night of great sex with Jay. She heard the door open and heard Tree walk in. She was thinking, *shit, are all these niggas so scared of him that one of them just couldn't kill him and spare me the trouble of having to pretend. Damn!* "Hey Baby, I missed you so much even though it was only two days."

She ran over, wrapped her arms around his neck and attempted to kiss him, but he pushed her away. She then noticed that Ish, Ice, and crazy-ass-trigger-happy, Evan, were standing behind him in the kitchen.

She looked at them and then at Tree. Smiling, she spoke, "Hey y'all, what's going on? Yo, Evan tell Renee to call me. I've been blowing up her phone and she ain't call me back. You must got her on lock, but please let her up for air so we can go shopping." Nina busied herself because deep down she knew something was not right for all them to be in her house, and for Tree to push her away like he did. "Y'all want something to drink? I got Heinekens and Coronas."

Still no one said a word. She noticed that Tree was no longer in the kitchen and had gone upstairs. "Y'all want to have a seat?"

Still, no word from anyone until Tree came down with a hand full of her clothes.

"Tree, baby, what are you doing with my shit?"

Tree nodded at Evan who said, "Nina your time here is up and you got to get your trifling ho-ass up out my man's crib. You can leave with whatever the man gives you to take back to Piedmont Projects or you can act like a chicken and try and cut a fool. It doesn't really matter, but your wife status has been terminated."

Nina looked at him and laughed and then at Tree, but no one was smiling. She ran over to Tree whose jaws were so tight she thought he would break his teeth.

He said, "If you touch me ever again you will be found bagged."

She tried to put on an act. "Baby, where is all this coming from? We have a life together…this is my fucking house Tree.

Tree snapped and grabbed her by the throat. "You thought I was a mother-fucking fool and you could do as you please, didn't you, Nina? You forgot that although I'm quiet, I run these streets. I am the mother-fucking man! Don't let shit fool you! You've been taking my money and giving it to Jay and then you're bold enough to have him in my house! Are you trying to die? Do you have a death wish? Well, while you were thinking you were smart and not banking your money because you were putting your eggs in Jay's basket, this nigga played you by having a wife and a new baby in Charlotte, lounging in a three-level house on two acres of land. Now fuck with that Nina. Bitch you lose...now bounce!"

Nina was standing in the kitchen stunned, unable to move. Could he just be saying this shit to hurt her? No, Jay would not do her dirty like that.

Tree smiled and said, "I know you think I'm bullshitting. So here Nina, I took the liberty of printing out the info on your man and his wife's marriage certificate. Nina took the paper and looked at it and couldn't believe her eyes, especially because of who was on record as being Jay's wife. Her own fucking sister. With that Nina passed out.

Chapter NINE

When Nina woke up she had a pounding headache and was hoping that the recent events she just went through were a dream. She rolled over, looked around and didn't see anything that looked familiar to her. She got up and felt a pain shoot through her vagina. She looked down and noticed her pants were not on and she was butt ass naked. What the fuck is going on? Then she heard a man's voice coming toward her and she panicked because nothing about the voice sounded familiar.

When the door opened, in walked a grungy-looking, older Hispanic man. "Oh Mommie, I see you're finally awake. I just left for a little while to get you something to eat and some aspirin since you kept saying your head hurts. I wasn't sure if your head was hurting because you were hungry or from the way I was hitting it doggy-style and you were throwing it back at me. Whichever it is, let me tell you, your pussy is like gold. I could stay up in it all night.

Nina backed away from the man and threw up. He attempted to run over to her but she just moved away again.

"Who the fuck are you and how did I get here? Where is

Tree?"

The man was now confused. "Remember I met you three days ago when you were standing out in the cold and said you had no money and no place to stay, and if I gave you a ride to the Piedmont you would gladly pay me anyway I wanted. I told you if you let me hit it I would call it even. Then you asked me to take you to get an 8ball first, we came here to my house and you've been here ever since."

Nina threw up again not believing her life was fucked up like this in less then a week.

The man went on to say his name was Juan and he had no clue who Tree was.

Nina asked, Did I have anything with me when you picked me up?"

"You had a bunch of clothes laying on the ground around you but that was it.

"Nina was starting to remember now how she ended up on the street broke and no place to go. Soon after Tree dropped a bomb on her about Jay and her sister she passed out, but with someone steady slapping her she had no choice but to come to. That's when she was pushed out of the car on the curb downtown and her clothes were thrown out of the car with her. Nina remembered sitting there crying and a cab pulling up. It had been years since Nina indulged in hard drugs but that night she needed what she knew always helped her cope and that was an 8ball. 8balls had been her way of survival growing up. It helped her escape when her mother was beating her ass. With only a choice of going back to her mother's house she thought the cab driver was a better option and offered herself.

Nina was furious. She asked Jun, "Do you have a phone? I need to make a call.

Juan handed her the phone and walked out of the bedroom to give her privacy.

Jay answered the phone sounding like he was still sleep. "Yo, who is this?"

"Tell me one thing and be a man, are you married to Shay?"

Jay yawned and sat up in the bed. "Why would you ask me some shit like that and why are you calling me from a strange number so early in the fucking morning? What's the problem Nina, you bored? Your man ain't around to nag? I mean what the fuck?"

"Just answer the question you bitch, are you married to Shay?"

Jay was getting a little sick of these females calling him a bitch and made a mental note when he saw Nina to bust her in her mouth. Suddenly Nina heard a baby crying.

"So it is true. You been fucking me and my sister the whole time and using me with no intentions of ever fully being with me."

Jay had had enough. "Yeah Nina, you found me out. I'm married to your sister and for the record, all shit don't run in the family because that wack-ass, used up, pussy of yours ain't saying nothing compared to you sister's. You know Tree is a joke thinking he the man and wifing a ho like you. But hey, you was good for what I needed now lose the number."

Nina could not believe this and wondered if her sister was in on this the whole time? Someone would pay for all of them playing her. She was not sure when or how but they would pay. Juan came back in the room with a look of concern and asked, "Are you OK?"

"Yeah, ummm, what did you say your name was?"

"Juan."

"Yeah, Juan, I am fine. I will be leaving soon and thanks again for allowing me to stay."

"Look, I don't know you, and not sure what's going on but if you need a place to stay you are welcome to stay here. The only thing I ask is no drugs in my home. The other night was an exception because you looked like you needed it or you would not make it, but I don't do drugs and don't like to be around it."

Nina told him she understood and yes, he was right, she did need it more then ever that night. Nina asked for the food he bought her and an aspirin. She ate like it was the last supper and passed out again. When she woke the sun was down. She called out for Juan but there was no answer. She got up and looked around at her new residence until she could come up with a plan to get Tree to forgive her and move back into their home. To her surprise, the house was nice and clean and not as bad as it could have been. There was a note on the dinning room table from Juan telling her he had left to go to work and if she needed anything just call him from the house phone. Her clothes were neatly folded in a pile on the couch. She found a tee shirt and sweats and thought a shower might clear her head. Nina attempted to call her sister a couple of times but didn't get an answer. This pissed her off so she left an ill message threatening her life. At this point, she was too tired to argue so she turned on the TV and curled up on the couch. Funny how life had turned full circle for her. She thought, *Damn, I am right back where I started.* She called Tree, but he had changed both the house and his cell number. *Damn! Now what?* If she could gauge his anger she might be able to come up with a lie to get him to believe. She was still trying to figure out how the hell he found out about Jay in the first place, and that she was giving him money. *Yeah Nina,* she thought, *you really fucked up this time.*

Chapter TEN

Tiffany was at work early because she had been gone for one day too many and she needed to do a lot of paper work and look over her books to make sure that everything was on the up and up. She sat back in her leather high back rocker behind her big mahogany desk and thought about Tree. She smiled because she just could not get him out her mind. *Hell, I am about to call his fine ass and see what he is up to*, she thought to herself.

"Hello."

"Hey Ma. I was just thinking about you. What's good? When can I see you?" He never beat around the bush about what he wanted.

"I'm working right now and not sure how long I will be here. Where are you?"

"I'm at the crib for the moment. I just got off the phone with the builder setting up a date to go down to look at the house because they are about finished.Plus I need to go check on something else down there for Von."

Tiffany was curious as to what that could be but decided not to be nosey right at this moment. "Well maybe we can get together when I'm done. I'll call and see what you're doing then. Will that work?"

"Yeah, but look Ma, I was wondering if you could fly out with me on Thursday to Atlanta to see the house? I'll be sure to have you back on Friday."

Tiffany loved the way he made her feel. She would go anyplace he asked, but decided to play it safe. "Well let me see what my schedule is looking like and I will let you know by Sunday, OK?"

"Yeah, that works. However you want to work it, it's your world, boss."

Tiffany laughed and promised she would call him in a few hours.

Tree took a shower, got dressed, grabbed his keys and headed toward the restaurant. He seated himself in the back, ordered a meal and checked out the crowd. When he finished he decided to chill there for awhile. His phone rang to *Forever My Lady* ring tone. That perked him up, knowing it was his lady. "Hey, Ma."

"Hey baby. I'm just finishing up. Do you think I could steal you away from your couch for a few?"

He laughed. "Are you still at the restaurant?"

"Yeah, I am, but I'm headed out the door in about two minutes."

Tree stood up and walked towards the door she would be walking out of. She was still talking on the phone, not knowing he was waiting by the door. When she opened it he grabbed her and attempted to kiss her but quickly pulled away remembering that she carried a razor in her mouth.

When she realized it was him she hit him and asked, "Are you crazy fool? I could have messed up that fine face with the shit you just pulled."

He laughed at her compliment. "Yeah, I am a little slow at times especially after eating that good food. I wasn't thinking at the time but I quickly came to my senses. You see I was fast on my feet."

She hit him on his shoulder and told him to bring his ass on. She grabbed his hand and led him out the door. Tiffany decided to drive him and he was not mad at that. They jumped into her 745 and headed toward the beach. She stopped to gas up. While Tree was pumping gas she made a quick call, reserved a room, and had them furnish the room with a couple bottles of Moet and fresh flowers. She always loved this hotel because some of the suites had their own private walk-out with a small pool outside the door. She planned to make good of the whole suite tonight and hoped her pussy was going to be able to stand the workout. Tree got back in the car and she headed toward the beach. He never even bothered to ask where they were going. He just leaned his seat back, closed his eyes and enjoyed the ride. When they pulled up to the hotel Tiffany had the car valet parked. Tree liked her style and liked that she was getting more comfortable with him, and going for what she wanted when it came to their relationship.

She checked in and they headed for the room both smiling at each other. Tiffany moved close to Tree in the elevator and began kissing him and rubbing him in sensitive places. Amused at how hard he had gotten so quickly, she reached over and hit the stop button on the elevator. While Tree was pumping gas, Tiffany had taken her thong off for easy access. She unbuckled his pants and pulled him out. His was woozy from the excitement and this was another first. She kissed him, bent over and backed up onto his dick. He slid into her with ease because she was so wet. He fit her like a hand in a glove and could not move at first. She slowly begin to grind and she instantly felt her juices flowing and felt the throb of his dick vibrating against her walls. Tree picked up his pace. He was sorry he wasn't going to make this a long session but the thrill of being in the elevator and the feeling of her pussy raw on his dick was driving him crazy. He felt himself hitting her spot and heard her moaning loader then usual. He bent over her back and whispered in her ear for her to come with him. She turned her head to the side, kissed him and asked if he was ready. He nodded his head yes, and they both came with each other.

After fixing themselves up a little, Tiffany hit the button and the elevator started back up. They jumped out and headed toward their room. When they stepped in Tree was impressed. She had really gone all out for a nigga. He had heard about the hotel but never had anyone that he really cared to bring to it, not even Nina. Tiffany jumped into the shower and he rolled a blunt. Later they sat by the pool and enjoyed each other.

"Tree, I want to experience sex in a hot tub for the first time and I want to do it tonight with you."

"Tiff I ain't going to fuck around with you because I want you to be my girl. I know I have only known you for a couple of weeks but I want you as my own now. If we get in this tub Ma, that's it. Your ass is on lock."

She looked into his eyes, read how serious he really was and saw no signs of him lying to her. Without another word, she dropped her towel, took his hand and led him to the hot tub.

Chapter ELEVEN

Diamond had been trying to get up with her cousin all evening to see what she was getting into. At first she was worried but when Von mentioned he was unable to get up with Tree, she knew what was up. It had been two months now and it seemed as though Tree and Tiffany were kicking it strong.

Tiffany usually got her hair done once a week and never missed an appointment. However, the last couple of weeks that Diamond had gone to Robbie to get her hair done her cousin wasn't there. Robbie asked Diamond if Tiffany was out of town on business or sick because Miss Thang never missed her standing appointment.

"Tell Tiffany she has a whole lot of explaining to do and he better be good when she explains it. If she's neglecting her hair for a lame man, she's going to hear it from me with no chaser."

Diamond said, Enough of your drama, get your ass back to work on my hair."

While she was under the dryer Tiffany called. She answered, "Bitch, being that I have been calling you the last three days, it better be good."

"Whoa…stop cutting up because it's you and Von's fault that I'm M.I.A. You should be finished with you hair in about an hour, right? I know that's where you are without asking, because you never miss your standing appointment. Meet me at Phillips for lunch."

Diamond agreed. "As long as it's going to be good gossip to go with that lunch."

Tiffany promised her it would. Before hanging up Diamond told her I should tell Robbie you're on this phone right now so he can cuss you out. On that, Tiff hung up because she knew her cousin was crazy enough to do it too.

At lunch Tiff told her cousin all about the time she spent with Tree when he wasn't traveling on business. She also told her about the house he was building, him asking her to consider moving and that he had practically moved into her condo because he was always there along with a lot of his stuff. She made a joke that he was trying to mark his territory or something because whenever he left he always managed to leave something behind.

Diamond asked about Nina and Jay. Tiffany filled her in on the drama with those two. Jay had put the word out that he would pay $10,000 for any information on the street about someone breaking into his house knowing he ain't got a dime left to his name. She wasn't sure what was going on but she had also heard that the last re-up that he got, he had been unable to move and now he was stressing because no money was being made. She told how Nina found out that Shay was married and had a baby with the very man who she was stealing for.

Diamond laughed so hard people turned around to see what was going on. She shot them a look that said *whatever*.

Tiffany calmed her down knowing that her cousin would cuss everyone in the restaurant out, and she was not in the mood for getting kicked out or having to back her cousin up in her Faliciano shoes. They continued on with the gossip. Tiffany told Diamond that Nina was working at Walmart and how she heard that she was living with some cab driver that was old enough to be her father, and has been in the club tricking…trying to find a baller. Word was out on the shit she tried to pull on Tree. Diamond had her mouth wide open and could not wait till she had an excuse to go to Walmart, and sure hoped that trick was working. She'd love to laugh in her face for trying to play family and thank her for being a lazy bitch and making it easy for her cousin to slide right in.

Tiffany did confide in her cousin that she wished Tree had a different profession because she wanted to be able to get all the way attached without worrying about the po-po coming to get her man. She told Diamond the man's dick game was so good that she lost focus on her promise not to date anyone in the game.

Diamond expressed that she understood more than a little where her cousin was coming from. She also told her that since she had finished school last month, Von was pressing her about going into a business of her own, and was also doing a whole lot of talking about moving south.

Tiffany was elated. "You need to move and come with me if I go with that nigga after all."

They talked for a while longer, hugged and went their separate ways. Tiffany stopped at the supermarket to get a few items for dinner because she knew Tree was coming into town. Although he told her it would be late, she figured she would have something in the microwave so he would have some home cooking after being on the road for a week.

Walking around in a daze thinking about her new found love, she felt someone staring at her. When she looked up it was Nina giving her the evil eye. Tiffany smiled at her and kept it moving, but today was just not her day.

"So Tiffany, how does it feel trying to play me and walk in my shoes?"

Counting to ten, Tiffany kept it moving in fear she would snatch that bitch up in the supermarket and then have to call someone down to central booking to bail her out.

Nina was not giving up that easy. "Yeah, while you think you got him I will always have him, I am wifey. As a matter of fact, he was just at my house two days ago. So I guess it is true what Jay said, the pussy is wack as hell because all the men you get always stray."

Before Tiffany knew it she had grabbed a can off the shelf and busted Nina in the face with it, then kept hitting her until some other customers came to Nina's rescue.

"Get the fuck off me and mind your own business before y'all are next. Nina, if you ever see me again in the street you'd better run because this shit ain't over. That was just a sample of what the rest of your ass whipping is going to be like times ten." Tiffany left her cart in the aisle while customers and store workers tried to attend to Nina. Tiffany knew it was best to get the hell out of dodge because she knew the police had been called. She picked up the phone and called Tree, but got no answer. She was furious he was not answering and she didn't even get her shopping finished. Tiffany decided she was going to leave his ass a message because she was not in the mood to deal with the bullshit, and if this is how it was going to be she was stepping.

When she arrived home she needed a bath to calm her nerves. She got her usual wine glass of her favorite wine and headed to the bathroom to get in the Jacuzzi. While relaxing her cell phone continued to ring, but she was in no rush to see who the caller was because it was her time. After getting tipsy in the tub, she lotioned her skin with La Prairie's Lotion , slipped into her silk night shirt and decided to lie down. She knew the candles would eventually burn out and she was loving the feeling of the glow it gave the room and was not ready to blow them out.

Tiffany drifted off to sleep and was awakened by the feeling of someone sucking on her toes and moving up her thigh with their hands. She open her eyes slightly, thinking she was dreaming, but felt a soft breeze slide across her clit and then felt one finger then two slide into her ever so gently. She opened her eyes again and focused on Tree. As mad as she had been, at that moment he was making up for the aggravation she had experienced at the supermarket with Nina. Tree was naked as he eased on top of her. Coming eye to eye with her, he planted soft kisses on her lips and whispered he was sorry for what he could not control, but all the drama would be over soon. She pulled him closer to her, sucked his tongue into her mouth and savored the taste of it. Tree had missed her even though it had only been a week and was ready to make a family with his woman. He made love to her that night like he had never done before and guessed he had never made love to anyone like that because he was never truly in love. He would never deny that he had love for Nina, but not the way a man was suppose to love his woman...not completely to the point were he lusted after her even when he knew she was his. No, loving Nina was because she made him feel wanted and needed. She depended on him and he loved to be able to take care of someone, plus he won't lie, her head game was out of this world.

The next morning when Tree woke up Tiffany was already gone. She left him a note saying she was happy he was home, she enjoyed his way of coming home, had really developed a lot of good feelings for him and hoped that it was not one-sided. She told him about a dream she had and that the more she thought about his proposal to move, the better it was sounding to her. The note said they would talk later and she truly loved him. Tree was touched and knew that the choice he and Von made was the best ever. But there were just a few loose ends that could not go without being taken care of.

Chapter TWELVE

Nina was furious and swore that she would get Tiffany's ass for breaking her nose and busting her eye. She was sick of all these women playing her and it was time to put payback into action. She had been working at Walmart and stripping sometimes to make ends meet. She moved out of Juan's house but whenever she needed something there was nothing he wouldn't do for her. Nina had become attached to Juan's care-giving ways and although they met on fucked up terms, she was happy he was in her life because if it had not been for his warm heart she would probably have been strung out someplace selling her body to cope with her sudden downfall in the game. She sat in her living room high off of pain killers with thoughts running through her mind of how she would seek revenge. She thought once she got those two bitches it would be payback enough for Jay and Tree. Yeah, they would feel her raft through the harm she would inflict on their women. All of them will be sorry for the day they ever met her.

Chapter THIRTEEN

Von and Diamond had been gone for two weeks and Tiffany was missing her sidekick. She was happy that they had gone on vacation to celebrate the news of becoming parents soon. Tiffany was so excited for her cousin and had already started looking through books, getting ideas on decorating the baby's room. Of course, the women in their family were so old fashion that they refused to shop for the baby until after the mother-to-be was in her fourth month, but Tiffany didn't care because she knew whatever was to be, would be. Look at her, she had made it to her fifth month and still lost hers. She was going shopping for the new baby regardless of a stupid belief.

She and Tree had gone south to see his house a couple of times in the last two months, and she was falling in love with it more and more. He had allowed her to talk with the builders, pick out counter tops and wall coloring. Tiffany was in her heaven, she loved to decorate. She always said she was going to start her own interior design studio to help those who had no clue. Her first client would be Tree. She smiled at the thought of the house and him. Tree had been gone a lot lately but he kept telling her it would soon be over. She was not sure when soon would be, but she hoped it was coming. Just then her phone rang and brought her out of her trance.

"Thank you for calling Savory, how may I help you?"

"Tiffany," a female said, crying hysterically. "This is Shay. Something has happened to Jay, he's in intensive care and they don't think he will make it."

Tiffany felt bad and could not believe her ears. But came to her senses and asked Shay, "Why are you calling me about your husband?"

Shay went on to explain that Jay owed a lot of people money and they let it be known that they would not stop till he was dead. They planned on collecting by any means including taking her and her baby out. Tiffany asked her if she knew the people and she said no. It's some Hispanic connect. She had never heard of him doing any business with them before, thought all his connects were with Von and Tree.

Tiffany told her that she knew nothing about it and there was nothing she could do, and asked that she not call her again.

Tiffany hung up and called Tree. He answered on the first ring. "Baby where are you?"

"Hello to you too, Ma."

"Sorry babe. I just got a call from Shay crying and shit about some Hispanic connects that did something to Jay and put him in intensive care and they're threatening her and the baby."

Tree was silent for a minute. "Tiff, why are them mother fuckers calling you about the shit? What you got to do with any of it?"

Tiffany was silent for a minute and then it dawned on her

that either they were trying to set her up or set Tree up. "I don't know now that I think about it."

Tree told her to stay by the phone. He needed to check on something right quick.

He called one of the girls in the barber shop over, asked her to call a number for him and ask to speak to Jay. When she called Jay's phone, the mother fucker answered. Tree thought this was a set up but why? Tree knew there was only one person, other then Von, he could trust without worrying and that was Cito.

Cito was like their father—he was the biggest drug lord in the North. No one crossed his ass and police, including the chief, let him run his shit because he kept them living comfortably. He was their employer and the city was just their part-time job. Cito had basically raised Von and Tree. He had no children and took them in as young boys when their fathers where killed in the streets. He molded them and taught them the meaning of loyalty. In return, when Von and Tree started their own crew, they made sure that their guys were not hurting in the streets and they instilled in their crew the value of using their money to start legal businesses to have whenever they decided to get out the game. In return they never had anyone turn on them.

Tree called his father, Cito. Cito answered the phone immediately and begin giving Tree the third degree. "Being that you're calling me boy, it must mean one of three things: you either got yourself in some shit, you're going to make me a grandfather or your brother is no place to be found."

Tree laughed. "Well Cito, one, I am going to bring her through to meet you and get your OK, but I already know you're going to love her; two, I do have a problem and last, yeah, Von is on a Caribbean island celebrating making you a grandfather.

Cito yelled, "Yeah, isn't that great! The old man can finally have someone to tear up the house and spend up his money."

Tree told Cito about all the events from meeting Tiffany to the foul shit with Jay and then the recent events of Jay and his wife trying to set-up Tiffany, but he couldn't figure out why.

Cito took it all in and said, You come see your father, boy…soon. And hey, bring my new daughter-in-law. Before hanging up he told Tree he was happy that he got rid of Nina because he never liked her, but his sons always have to do things their way.

Tree knew that his father changed the subject because he was not one to talk business on the phone. With that he told Cito he would be there by noon tomorrow. He called Tiffany back and told her to make sure she was ready, he was taking her to meet his mentor, his dad.

Chapter FOURTEEN

Nina found out that Jay would be out of town on business for a few weeks and it was as good a time as any to set her plan into motion. With Juan's help she had saved money to put all her works into action. She had him purchase her a burner, telling him it was for her safety since she lived alone. She also told him that she wanted to go to Charlotte to visit her mother and sister.

Juan said, "I thought your mother lived here in the projects?"

She said, "She does but I consider my sister's mother more of a mother then mine. She gave him a sob story about her life, he crumbled and purchased the ticket for her. She flew south first class and for the first time in months, felt she was living the life she used to with Tree. She had been on the internet at the library and was able to get her sister's address. It didn't hurt that she knew her sister's social security number and she also called Duke Power just to verify that the address she got off the internet was legit.

When she pulled up in her rental, she broke down crying because she could not believe that Jay had deceived her and instead, placed her sister in the beautiful house he'd promised her. When Nina got herself together she walked up to the house but decided to go to the back. What do you know… her sister was so cozy in her new place she had left the back door open. Nina peeped in, saw no signs of her sister, pulled her gun out and walked into the house. She walked around and found her sister sitting in the nursery with the baby. She stood there for a while and finally her sister looked up.

Startled she asked, "What are you doing in my house?"

Nina laughed and said such attitude, "Aren't you happy to see your sister?"

Shay said, Look Nina, whatever beef you have is with you and Jay. I'm sick of the both of y'all."

Nina looked at her and then at the baby and said, "Well I guess what they say about blood being thicker then water ain't true after all huh, sister?"

Shay laid the baby down unfazed that her sister was holding a gun. Truth be told, the only reason she put up with the shit was because of her son. Otherwise, she would have been out and would've left Jay to Nina or Tiffany to deal with. She just wanted her son to have the finer things in life, but the more she thought about it the more it was not even worth it.

"Look Nina, why are you here?"

Nina said, "Oh, now you want to talk, huh? Well let's see. You're supposed to be my sister and yet you helped this man play me. Hell…you played me, so I guess I am here now to get my revenge on all those that sent me back to the projects and put my life in rewind mode to where the fuck I started."

She was so angry she walked up to Shay and hit her repeatedly. Shay just took it and laughed. Nina was confused as to why her sister did not even try to defend herself.

Shay looked at her and said, "Bitch, that's all you got? You so busy complaining about what people did to you and what man you don't have...you're a fucking joke. You want Jay, bitch, you can have him and all the shit that comes along with it—STD's, ass whippings, women calling your house, other babies—you can have him! Just help me pack my shit!"

Nina looked at her sister in shock. This was not going as planned.

"Look Shay, enough of your sob story. You're trying to play mind games and I ain't for it. Now what I want you to do is call that bitch, Tiffany, and make her believe something is wrong with Jay. Get her to come down here."

"Bitch, you're crazy! That girl is not checking for Jay's shit. She was smart enough to have left his ass and she's done!"

Nina hit her sister again and threw the phone at her. After placing the call and Nina's plan not working, just like Shay said, Shay looked at her and asked, "Why you fucking around? You know Tree going to hear about this and when he does, your ass is good as dead for fucking with that girl."

Nina heard enough and fired off a shot at Shay leaving her laid out right in her son's nursery.

G STREET CHRONICLES
A NEW URBAN DYNASTY

WWW.GSTREETCHRONICLES.COM

Chapter FIFTEEN

Tiffany and Tree went up to Cito's lake side estate. Tiffany could not close her mouth. The land and the home were so beautiful. She had only really seen places like this in magazines. She had been around money, but this was beyond money—this was like a dream.

After Cito met Tiffany he immediately welcomed her into La Familia. He gave her a tour of the house, stopped at one room and said this is yours to decorate for my grandchild.

Tiffany smiled and said, "Oh, you can't wait either for Von and Diamond's baby? Me either. And I would love to decorate it. There is so much I can do to this room."

Cito said, "No, their baby's room is right next to this one, but you can do that one too. No, I'm talking about your baby with my son, Tree."

Tiffany felt a little uncomfortable and tried to change the subject. Cito was wise in his years, and although his wife was now dead she had been pregnant three times. She never gave birth but he knew a pregnant woman when he saw one. I know Tree didn't want to steal the shine from his brother's announcement but he could have told me.

Tiffany said, "I'm sorry sir, but you must be mistaken me for another one of his women."

Cito laughed so hard he shook a little. He explained to her about being able to spot a pregnant woman when he saw one. He said I told Diamond she was pregnant before she knew she was pregnant. Tiffany thought for a while and realized that she had not had a period in the last month. Her face became flushed and she had to sit down. Tree went over and asked if she was OK.

She said, "I'm fine. I just needed to sit for a minute, but I'm fine." She smiled, stood up, straightened her clothes, and continued the tour, never looking again into the room Cito deemed as her baby's room.

After the house tour Tree and Cito went into the office and talked business. Cito had told her to make herself at home and do anything she would do at home. She busied herself moving furniture around and rearranging stuff to keep busy while thoughts of being pregnant ran through her mind. On one hand she was happy, but on the other she was scared. What if history repeated itself and Jay was right about her insides being all fucked up?

"Cito, I think I'm ready to move on with life and get out the game. I believe we are square and I don't want to block your money. I've been thinking hard and I want to pass my blocks and territory over to Ish. He has been with me since day one and he has never crossed me. Not once has Ish complained about anything and his money has always been on point. I tested Ish like you taught us to do to see how he handled family bonds. He passed with flying colors."

Ish had done a pick-up for Tree and the supplier gave him way more products saying it was a sign of thanks. Ish could have taken the extra and not told me shit about it, but instead he called while standing there with the supplier and explained what the supplier had added.

"I have never let him know but I've been grooming him. He now owns two barber shops and a printing press." He went on to tell Cito that he invited Ish up to the house to hand over his share to him today. Even though Tree was not sure about Cito's comment about the baby, he knew he was done.

Tree waited for Cito's response and finally he spoke. "So I'm losing both of my sons to the game?"

"No Cito, we are just out of La Familia business. We are your sons for life and we ride with you till the end."

Cito was moved because he always thought that once the boys left the life they would leave him. He thought the only reasons the boys were true to him was because he taught them the game and supplied them for the low. Without them in the game he thought their bond was over. Cito got up, came around the desk and hugged Tree, giving him his blessings.

Tree looked at Cito and said, "Wait, you said both of you sons are out the game."

Cito looked away and said, "Oh, it must be a mistake."

Tree laughed and said, "No old man you meant it. So my brother, Von, has been to talk to you?"

Cito said, "Don't be upset with your brother. We were to have a Committee meeting when he gets back and we were going to tell you then."

Tree smiled and said, "It's cool Cito, we have been talking about it for a while and I've been trying to get that nigga to get out, so I am happy he is. I don't care if I am the last to know or not."

Just then the door bell rang and they ended their meeting to see who it was. Ish came in and greeted everyone a little nervous as to why he had been called to the big boss' house. Ish knew he had never crossed anyone…he had been loyal.

Tree smiled at him and said, "Relax, when it's all over you'll be happy."

Cito took Ish into his office and Tree said he would be right in he just wanted to check on Tiff. "Hey Ma, you OK? You seem to pretty quiet the last hour or so."

When he walked fully into the room where she was he smiled because she had done her thing in the room. It was totally different than when they first got there. He could not believe it was the same room. The maid came in, told Tiffany her lunch was ready and asked her if she could show her a couple of pictures of her living room for some ideas. Tiffany kissed Tree on his cheek and walked off with the maid to eat and talk.

Tree joined Cito and Ish and they got down to business. When their meeting was over Ish could not believe that his loyalty and patience had paid off. He was now the boss. He would be taking Tree's place. Ish asked who was taking Von's spot and Cito told him Von would chose a person upon his return, and if he didn't then Ish was the man of it all. Tree felt it only right to celebrate and called the club to set it up for Saturday, because he knew Von would be back Thursday and would want to help bring Ish in right.

During their drive home from Cito's, Tree never mentioned anything about Tiffany being pregnant and she was thankful because she was not in the mood to talk about it. He dropped her at home saying he would be back after running a few errands. She decided then to make a quick trip to Rite Aid to pick up a pregnancy test. Since Tree wouldn't return for a while, it was now or never to know.

She went into the bathroom, took the test but was reluctant

to look at the results. She had been sitting in the bathroom over an hour when Tree returned to her condo. He walked through the house looking for her and found her on the tub, seemingly incoherent. He called her name a couple of times and bent down in front of her without her ever looking up at him, just continuing to stare into space. He noticed the pregnancy test in her hands and saw in the window 'pregnant'. He was overjoyed but maintained his cool. He lifted her off the end of the tub, carried her to the bed and lay laid next to her.

"Tiff, talk to me babe, how long have you been in there, and why didn't you call me?" He held her close to his chest and felt tears coming down her face. "Tiff, you don't want to have a baby with me? What's up Ma, say something you're making me nervous."

Tiffany finally pulled herself together and was able to speak, but it came out in a whisper. "Tree, I'm scared. What if this time I can't carry this baby like the last? What if Jay is right?"

Tree tensed up because he wanted to fuck Jay up, better yet bag his ass for putting that thought in her head. "Look baby, some things are meant to be. Us, our child, our future together is meant to be. It was designed for us. So I need you to stop worrying and please stop crying before you make me hurt someone. Now let's call and make a doctor's appointment before you get all ahead of yourself."

His smile showed those beautiful dimples, and it made her smile. She decided he was right and put all the bad thoughts out her mind.

Chapter SIXTEEN

Word spread that Shay had been shot to death and found in her son's room. The worst of it was the baby was missing. Jay was furious and vowed that he was going to make Tree and Von pay for what they were doing to him. First he was robbed then his wife killed and now he had no clue as to where his first born child, his son, was. Shit had gone down hill. Jay thought this was not the work of someone from Charlotte because he had not gotten his feet wet good enough to upset or step on anyone's toes there. No this shit was personal and had Maryland written all over it. Not to mention he had gotten word from some of his homeboys that Tree had put the word out for no one to fuck with him. Yeah, it was time to move back and settle a score with a couple of people he knew who never wanted him to succeed. They will be sorry once he got a crew up, that they ever messed with Jason Wells, a/k/a Jay.

* * *

After coming back from their doctor's appointment,

getting the good news that everything so far with the pregnancy looked good and Tiffany was in fact, eight weeks pregnant, she was more than excited. She laid down to take a nap but couldn't wait until later to pick up Diamond and Von at the airport to tell them their children would be growing up together. Tree could not stop smiling and planned to take serious what the doctor said about her being easy and not working and stressing about things during the next couple of months. His first thought was to make sure he found someone to run the normal day-to-day of the restaurant until they made more definite plans about moving. He knew now that they were planning a family, and the fact that he was almost officially out the game, she could not resist his offer to start their family in the south, in the home he was building.

Tree's phone rang and brought him out of his thoughts quickly. He looked at the caller ID and saw it was the club owner. "Hello Raja, how are things coming along for the party tomorrow?"

"Everything is good Mr. Douglas. I just wanted to confirm that you would be bringing the guest list in today so that we will have it at the door for tomorrow night. I also wanted to go over everything you ordered to make sure the party is how you want it."

They were on the phone for a good hour going over things from the liquor to the lighting to ice sculptures and adult entertainment for the male guests in a private room and booths. When all the party business was finalized, he checked to see if Tiffany was up from her nap and ready to head to the airport.

When he walked into their room Tiffany was staring out the window. "What's wrong?"

"Nothing really, I am happy but scared at the same

time. I know I am not supposed to be stressing but I can't help it. I have been giving a lot of thought to moving and I have decided that I am going to sign the restaurant over to my brother. He will be good as an owner. Hell, hotel and restaurant management was his major in college and, of course, if he needs me I will only be a phone call away. So what do you think?"

"I think it's a good idea. It will be another two months before the house is completed and as long as you promise to take it easy, I think it would be great to get your brother in on it now so you can show him the ropes and get him comfortable with the whole thing before we leave."

Tiffany smiled and said, "I figured you would feel that way."

She got up, put on her Coach sneakers, grabbed her matching purse and they headed out the door.

Chapter SEVENTEEN

It had been a month now since Nina moved out of Maryland to Florida with her new son. Nina played a good role at being a mother. She was able to land a job at a local insurance company as a title agent and built a whole new life for herself. All her new found friends and co-workers believed that shortly after having her baby, the child's father was killed and she had to move to get away from all the bad memories. So far the lie had been working for her. And while she was working on a new life she didn't forget her promise to get even with all those in Maryland who had wronged her. Nina still thought about Jay a lot especially because his son looked just like him. She thought of her sister at times too, but then erased her out of her mind because she justified that her sister was not really her sister if she could deceive her like she did. Nina called Jay one time after the murder and he was so broken up about the death of Shay and his missing son that was all he could talk about. She tried to seem compassionate but was pissed off because she didn't want to hear about his little family, she wanted to hear about them. She really was hoping that he would beg for her forgiveness and want her back. Unfortunately, he didn't, so let his ass suffer without his son.

After some time, Nina thought more about Jay and figured what the hell, it's been a while, let me call and see if he's talking different.

"Yeah, who dis?"

"Hey you. It's me, Nina. I had you on the brain so I figured I would call."

"Oh shit, Nina, what's up baby? Long time no hear from. Where you've been hiding yourself since I've been back home? I've been asking people about you but no one says they've seen you."

Nina was at a loss of words for a minute, and was not sure she had heard him correctly when he said he was back home in Maryland.

"Hello Nina, you still there?"

"Oh, I'm sorry Jay. Anyway, did you say you are back home?"

"Yeah, I got back a month after all that shit went down. I've formed a crew and I'm trying to get back on. Baby when you going to hang with a nigga for old times sake? I mean where you at so I can come scoop you? We need to talk and I need to apologize and make things right between the two of us, you heard?"

"Well Jay, that sounds good and all but I moved out of state. I wanted to tell you before but with my sister's death and then the way things went down, I never got a chance to tell you."

"Damn, so that means it's a wrap for me and you then huh, lil lady?"

"I wouldn't say that, I just needed to get my head together, you know?"

"Yeah, I feel you and like I said, I am really sorry how shit went down and I want to make it up to you and possibly try us again, you know?"

Nina was holding the phone so tight she almost broke it. Her mind's wheels were going a mile a minute and she was conflicted with what to do, whether to believe his ass or continue with her plan. She figured she would go along with the plan and see what happened. Worst case she always had her plan A to fall back on.

"Well Jay, what's going on this weekend? There's an e-saver into Maryland. Maybe I can come spend the weekend and we can catch up and go from there."

"Yo, that sounds good. You need me to send you the money?"

"No, I'm good, I got it."

"Well look, make sure you pack something hot because they're throwing a party for Ish tomorrow on some real VIP shit, and I plan on letting niggas know I'm back in town, and it wouldn't hurt to have you on my arm just to make shit official and throw salt in Tree's face."

Nina smiled and asked, "Why are they were having a party for Ish? Is it his birthday or something?"

"Naw, you ain't heard Tree and Von done handed the business down to Ish? They haven't selected a second leader but this Ish coming out party."

"Oh, for real? Well, like I said, after I heard of my sister's death I just up and moved away from everything and everyone. You know even though what y'all did was foul, she was still my baby sister."

Jay was quiet for awhile, partially because he ain't give two shits about how Nina was feeling because he knew whatever happened to his wife and child had something to do with her because she moved right afterward. And second, because he had some young tender sucking his dick while they were in the truck and he was on the phone.

"Yo, Nina, hit me tomorrow and let me know when your flight gets in. I got to go take care of something."

"OK, I'll book the flight and give you a call."

"Yo, come over here and jump on this dick, you got me hard as a rock." With that he pushed his seat back and enjoyed the ride.

* * *

Nina decided to make a phone call to Octavia because she knew whatever gossip the hood had she would know. "Yo, what's up? Tavia, this Nina, bitch, what's good?"

"Oh shit, where the hell you been with your trick ass?"

Nina burst in laughter because Octavia was crazy as hell. "Girl, I came down here to Florida with this balla dude I met in Jersey, and we been down here chilling and shopping hard girl. I will be flying home tomorrow."

"Oh shit, I hear that chick. Why you ain't hook me up with one of his boys or some shit girl. I told you about that stingy shit didn't I?"

"I know, but I was out that night, we had a good time and the next morning he called and said he wanted me to fly out with him, but don't pack nothing. So I went. I ain't know I was going to be gone this long."

"OK. Well, I'll let you slide."

"Well thank you. So what's been good in the hood?"

"Girl you done missed all the latest. Tavia sat back and put her feet up with a glass of E & J and a blunt and put Nina down on the hood chronicles. OK. First, Jay done moved back and he living over here in Piedmont projects and getting a crew up. He got a couple of young boys on his team so far and he been getting a little change out here. Von and Diamond, girl, about to have a baby. And girl, your boy, Tree, done lost his mind. Handed all that money he be making over to Ish to make. He out the game girl!!! Can you believe that shit? Word on the street is that stuck up ho of his, Tiffany, talked him out the game. I don't know what the fuck wrong with her because when I say he is a major figure and getting that money. I would never want my man to stop. Oh and get this! Are you sitting down girl?"

"Yeah, Tavia, I'm sitting down. What's up?"

"Tree bout to have a baby with that trick."

Nina dropped the phone.

"Nina, girl you still there?" Octavia knew that would affect her so she saved it for last. "Nina!!"

"Yeah, I'm here girl." The phone slipped out my hand when I was reaching for my suitcase.

Octavia smiled because she knew that was a lie. They talked for another hour and then promised to get up with each other tomorrow at Ish's party. Nina could not believe this shit. The whole time she was with Tree's ass he always told her he ain't want no children. But he gets with that bitch and after a year they are having a baby. Hell no! She might be pregnant but that baby will never be born. But first she had to get rid of Jay's baby boy, Jayshawn.

Tiffany and Diamond shopped all day Saturday, trying to find something hot to wear to the party. They also were catching up on the two weeks they had been away from each other. "Tiff, you and Tree will have to go to Saint Lucia before you have the baby. Girl, it was like something you only see in the books but don't believe that the pictures are really real.

Like maybe they airbrush them or something."

Tiffany laughed. "Girl, with so much stuff going on with me trying to get your rock head cousin, Lil Mike, situated with the restaurant, the news of the baby and flying back and forth with this house, I don't know when we would find the time."

Diamond figured now was a good time as any to tell her cousin the other good news that they would actually be neighbors. Before they left for their honeymoon Von surprised her with the blueprints to their new house.

"Tiff, I didn't get a chance to tell you before I left, Von gave me a wedding gift that I guess was half for me and half for you."

Tiffany was confused. "What could he possibly give you Diamond that would be a gift for the two of us? You know I do not get down like that. I could throw up right now just thinking about Von in that manner."

"Girl, stop. You my cousin and all, but I would kill your ass first before I shared him with you." They both had a good laugh on that. "Anyway, little nasty, we are going to be neighbors!"

"Diamond, I told you I made the choice to move to Atlanta with Tree."

"You know Tiff, I always told your mother and Nana you were slow but, damn, you're really proving my point this time. Me and Von, you following me so far?"

"Yeah, you and Von what?"

"Are moving to Atlanta and he bought the land next to you and Tree. Now do you understand with your slow minded self?"

Tiffany started jumping up and down in the middle of the mall, dropped her bags and hugged her cousin. "This calls for a drink!!! Let's go."

"Hold your horses, we can't drink. Shit, we're both pregnant."

"Oh shit! Yeah, I forgot. OK well let's go pick out some shoes, we've got to celebrate somehow. Wait, I got to call Tree and tell him, although he probably already knows."

Chapter EIGHTEEN

Nina purchased a ticket for herself and Jayshawn. She had been up all night trying to come up with a plan to get Jay back with his son, and also how to get close enough to Tiffany to make Tree pay. Nina had decided that she would drop him off at a hospital in Charlotte, with a note attached, and then fly to Maryland and reunite with Jay. She got to Maryland at 11 that morning, and when she walked out of the airport Jay was leaned against his black-on-black with black tint, 22" rims, Yukon. She smiled because he was still fine as hell. Time was truly on his side and it seemed money was not an object anymore to him either. She ran up to him and hugged him. He hugged and kissed her and told her she looked good. She did really look good, but he knew she was dirty as hell too.

"Yo, jump in, let's go shopping."

"Sounds good baby, let's go."

Jay decided to take a trip to Philly to shop so that he had on some fly shit he was sure no one else would have. It was going to be a good night for him, he just knew it. Nina was in her own thoughts and plans but she would ride the shit out with Jay. On the ride back to Jay's place to get ready, he decided to see if he had pull like back in the day. He pulled over at a rest stop and asked, "Nina, baby, you still got it like you use to?"

"Shit, you know skills can only get better, not worse."

With laughter, she lifted up, took her thong off and handed it to him. He sniffed them like he use to and smiled at her.

"You want to taste the product first?"

"I don't mind if I do."

Sticking two fingers in her now wet pussy, she took them out and stuck them in his mouth. He sucked on her fingers like they were a popsicle, and began to moan with the sweet taste resting on his tongue.

"Damn baby, don't make a nigga wait, get on this dick and ride out."

Nina had other plans. She reached over, unbuttoned his pants, reached in and pulled his big black, rock hard, eight inches out. She always wondered, as cocky as he was why his dick was not at least ten inches. He always pleased her, but at that moment all that flashed in her mind was Tree and the sex they use to have when they first met. Nina bent down and rubbed her lips across the tip of his dick. Jay leaned his head back and closed his eyes. She licked down the length of his dick and went to his balls, put them in her mouth and played with them softly on her tongue. Licking back up the length of his dick, she took the whole thing in her mouth and it almost felt like she had swallowed his whole dick down her throat. Jay was gone. The one thing he always remembered is no one, even if he lied and said they did, could fuck with her head game. Jay tried to pull her up but it was too late, he had blasted off all down her throat. Nina laughed, wiped her mouth, and said I think we need to get back on the road and get ready if you're making that party tonight. Jay was exhausted and wanted to go to sleep after that nut, but he fixed his pants, started up the truck and headed south bound on I–280.

That night the club was jumping and packed with the who's who of the hood. Some of the Baltimore Ravens had come through because they were in town for a game with Knicks and in full effect at the party. Even a few celebrities had shown up to show Ish some love. Tiffany and Diamond were in heaven, just happy to get their party on, and a good one at that, because they knew it would be a long time before they would be able to party again. Tree, as usual, was posted up in the corner watching people that had not even noticed he was present. Tiffany had not been paying attention till she realized that Tree had not been near her within the last hour. She finally spotted him and went to make sure he was OK.

"Baby, why you ain't over there having fun and welcoming Ish into his new position in the game?"

He hugged her close to him and said you know Von is the party boy...I just watch and listen. You know how I do, this how you met me."

Tiffany remembered and said, "This is very true and as weird as you looked, you were so fine I just had to meet you."

They both laughed, but Tree stopped abruptly when he noticed Jay and Nina walking in. Tiffany looked up at him and followed his eyes to see what he was looking at. She could not believe her eyes but, at the same time, she was wondering how the fuck they got up in there. Jay walked around giving out pounds, eventually making his way to Ish and hugging and congratulating him. Ish looked from him to Nina, nodded his head and went back to talking to the people around him.

Jay extended his hand to Von and Von looked at him and laughed. "Man don't play yourself. You know we ain't cool."

Jay said, "Man that shit's old, let bad blood be. By the way, congrats on the new family man, I wish you better luck than I had with mine."

A slight grin crept across his face and Nina knew he had crossed the line. Jay turned to walk away and Von banged his ass in the back of the head with his gun. Jay bent over in pain but Von was far from finished. Von kicked Jay in the face and when Jay hit the ground, Von continued to kick and hit him. Nina went to defend Jay, but Diamond was right on her. Nina knew Diamond would defend her man, and when Diamond got within punching distance Nina punched her dead in the stomach. Diamond bent over in pain and Nina kicked her in the leg until Diamond went to the ground in pain. Once she was down Nina lifted up her leg to stomp her in the stomach. Tiffany came up behind her unexpected and cut Nina right on her knee leaving her no choice but to join Diamond on the ground screaming in pain. Tiffany helped her cousin up and made her way to the door. Diamond was screaming in pain.

"Hold on D, it's going to be OK, just hold on."

Before Tiffany knew it, she heard gun shots go off and was praying Tree and Von would be OK. Tree's car was right at the door. Crying hysterically, Tiffany got Diamond in the car, picked up her cell phone and screamed in it for Lil Mike to meet her at the hospital now. She hung up and accelerated to about 80 MPH to the hospital. Tiffany pulled up to the emergency room and ran inside screaming for help. Nurses and doctors ran out and got Diamond on a stretcher.

"Miss, you have to move your car or it will be towed."

"Fuck you, you move it then." Tiffany threw the security guy the keys and ran inside.

Lil Mike walked in on the phone, looking around for Tiffany. "Yo, Tiff what the fuck is going on?"

"There was a fight at the club and Nina hit Diamond in the stomach and kicked her. I got to her just before she stomped on her stomach and cut her ass in the knee. The baby just got to be OK, Lil Mike. If it's not, I ain't responsible."

Just then Mike's phone rang and he saw on the called ID it was Tree.

"Yo nigga were you at?"

"We down here at Regional. They got Diamond in the back. Yo, where the fuck Von at?"

"We on our way, I got him in the car with me now."

When Tree and Von arrived, Tiffany broke down again and asked what the fuck happened and where were the damn off duties they had hired to keep the fucking peace. This shit was not supposed to happen. The whole time Tiffany was going off, Von never said a word. He had not said anything the whole ride there either.

"Mr. Erickson?"

"Yes, that's me. How's my wife?"

"She will be fine. I'm keeping her overnight to monitor the baby and make sure the bleeding stops."

"Bleeding? Doc, what are you talking about?"

"Evidently during the altercation your wife said she was involved in, she was hit in the stomach. That caused some aggravation which caused her to bleed a little from some tearing inside. We are keeping her overnight to make sure that is where it was coming from and nothing else. If that's the case, she will heal fine and it will not affect the baby at all. She will need to have doctor visits at least twice a week for the next two months, and a lot of bed rest. Other than that, I believe she will have a healthy pregnancy. Are there any questions?"

"No. Doc, can I just see my wife please?"

"Sure. They are cleaning her up now and a nurse will come get you after she's moved to her room."

Tiffany was sitting in a chair rocking and praying the entire time the doctor was talking. Von sat down to wait, holding his head in hands. It wasn't long before the nurse came out to get him. Before walking to the back he stared at Tree for a long time looking for reassurance that all was well. Tree nodded his head, lifted Tiffany up and walked out the hospital.

Chapter NINETEEN

Two days later, Diamond was discharged and re-turned home. Tiffany refused to leave her side. Von slept in the guest room because Tiffany insisted on sleeping in his room with her cousin. Diamond confided in Tiffany what she was feeling when she thought she was going to lose the baby and, of course, Tiffany could fully understand everything. A knock at the door briefly interrupted their conversation and the tears started again. Von had flown Diamond's mother to Maryland from Charlotte to keep an eye on her and keep her in check. Diamond was so happy to see her mother she held on to her until she was able to stop crying. Tiffany was crying too because her mother was right behind her aunt.

"What is this, have they called the wardens in on us?"

"Hell yeah, because apparently y'all don't know how to sit down and be pregnant."

The room was full of laughter and tears. If wasn't long before the mothers decided to hit the kitchen to cook up a down home meal for everyone.

Nina woke up a week later in ICU and was scared to death

because she couldn't remember how she got there. A nurse noticed she was awake and called the doctor.

"Well young lady, nice of you to join us. You slept for about a week. You were brought in by ambulance after a car crash."

Nina looked at the doctor, then the nurse and whispered Jay's name. The nurse checked her vitals while the doctor looked over her chart.

"Well Mrs. Fields, that is your name right? We were informed that you were in a car crash and the car caught fire. A person passing by was able to get you out the car before it blew up. We're sorry to inform you that your husband didn't make it."

Nina opened her mouth to scream but nothing came out. Nina could not believe that she was almost killed by Von and Tree. The doctor ordered the nurse to give her a sedative. When it kicked in, Nina drifted off to sleep and woke up two days later to the sound of a familiar voice. She focused on a male figure and tried reaching for the call button, but was slower than her guest.

"Hi Nina, happy to see you're awake. I've been here on and off for the past week and a half."

Nina was scared to death because she knew he was there to finish her off since she made it out alive. She tried to say something but he talked over her.

"Look, if it was not for me pulling you out of the burning car, you would be dead. I saved you. I've been here watching over you since then. I'm not here to hurt you. I've always had feelings for you from when we were in high school together, but you were so busy chasing the dollar to survive, you were not checking for a nigga on the come up. I understand and all because I know how your home life was, but I've always been here. How do you think you ended up at Juan's house and he was able to take care of you on a cabbies salary? That was me. I made him promise to never tell and it would be all good. I wanted you to come to me on your own, but then you skipped town. By the way, I have Jayshawn at my mother's. See, I was also there that day you took your sister out. I was there to pay Jay a little visit for the shit he did to you, I didn't know you were as gansta as you are, so I was in shock when I walked in the nigga's crib after you rolled out, and saw your handy work on your own sister."

Nina was in shock. All this time he had been looking out for her and she never knew.

"Look, I got a crib set up for you in VA. I want you to stay there and be low-key while I take care of some shit. I hope you trust me, but if you don't tell me now and I will have you on a flight back to where you came from."

Nina closed her eyes and began to cry. After awhile, she was able to see him clearly and he extended his arms to hold her.

"Ishmael, after all I've been through why you just now coming to me?"

"I had to get something in the works. I knew that Tree and Von was getting out the game and Boo, I was loyal to them mother fuckers even when they were greedy with the money. I had put in the work, and I wanted to come to you with the kingdom. I was not sure when Tree was talking bout retiring that I was going to get the crown. And if I had not, I was ready to fight for it, but it worked out. Now I know you got some ill feelings for those niggas and some shit you want to handle, and I'm ready to ride with you now to get your revenge. I am the MAN! I got the crew and I got the money getting ready to roll in…I am fucking unstoppable and together we can make this shit bigger than they ever had it. You willing to ride with me Nina?"

"How I know you ain't setting me up and you ain't still working with them?"

"If I was I would have just killed your ass while you were in the coma and been done."

"Well, how did you end up with Jayshawn?"

"The night I was to set the car on fire, Jay's phone rang and it was the hospital in Charlotte. I pretended to be him. I flew out with a fake ID, got him, and came right back to be with you."

Nina was at a loss for words for the first time. "Look Nina, I need you to check yourself out the hospital tomorrow morning. I will be here to pick you up and take you to the crib in VA. If you're here too much longer, it is bound to get out that you're still alive."

Nina nodded her head and leaned on Ish hoping that everything he had said was true, and not a set-up to torture and kill her.

Chapter **TWENTY**

With her aunt and mother there, Diamond thought she was going to lose her mind. She was horny as hell and wanted to get out and have some fun. She had tried several times to go shopping, but her mother wasn't trying to hear it.

"Tiff what's up?"

"Nothing girl, just sick of being in the house. How are you feeling?"

"I'm fine, still sore in some spots, but this house arrest is for the birds. I feel like I've been put in prison for a crime I didn't commit."

"Yeah, because of you I have been placed on lockdown. But it's cool because from what I heard last night, they're planning to leave in a couple of days and you know once they leave, I'm back on the street."

"Yeah, whatever. Till Tree gets a hold of that ass."

"You're probably right, but let's make plans to go to DC and New York the following week to do baby shopping."

"Girl, I've been on-line and found furniture I absolutely love at Baby and Me Boutique. I told Von to check it out for me, but he's been so busy. He keeps promising me he'll get to it. Tiff, did you hear they found Jay dead in a car? It appears that he had a wreck."

"Diamond, he had a wreck alright, he crossed the line and got served a death sentence. Have you heard anything about Nina?"

"No girl. I asked Tree and all he says is he doesn't want to talk about it. He, Von and Ish have been here for the last 2 hours, having a meeting downstairs in the office. I passed it a couple of times, but could only get bits and pieces. It sounds like she's alive, but they are not sure how she made it out of the crash and where she is."

"Damn, this could have all been avoided if she would have just stayed under the rock she was under."

"But Diamond, here is the other kicker. Last night Tree was on the phone with Evan and you will not believe this, so I hope you are sitting down. It appears that she moved after she killed her sister and kidnapped her baby! Jay ain't know shit about it, that they know of, so I guess that's why he was flossing her that night. But this chick is crazy. How you going to kill your own sister over a man? I just hope that wherever she is, she stay there and just be done with Maryland for good."

Diamond was in shock. She thought to herself, *this chick went after her, tried to kill her baby, and had also killed her own sister. How ruthless can a bitch be?* "Damn Tiff, that shit is deep. Anyway, I don't want to talk about it no more because it's depressing just thinking about that night and how I could have lost my baby. By the way, I go for my ultrasound tomorrow. You want to go? I'll find out what the sex is. You know a bitch nosey and cannot wait till I give birth to know."

Tiffany laughed and said, "It makes no sense that you have no patience."

"Oh shut up bitch, because when next month rolls around, you're going to want to know too." Tiffany knew her cousin a little too well.

"Yeah, I will check with the warden to see if I can get a pass or if she can at least drive me there."

"Is Von going?"

"I don't know yet. He's being a real crab these days and he's withholding the sex. He's trying to use the excuse that he wants to wait till the doctor gives the OK, but shit, Miss Kitty ain't trying to hear all that. When he hugs me Tiff, my pussy starts flipping! Shit, I have to look down sometime to make sure she ain't jump up out the panties and run across the floor looking for water to cool her down."

Tiffany almost peed on herself laughing so hard. "Well cousin, I can't say that I feel your pain because I've been getting rocked to sleep every night for the past two weeks. And not to rub it in or nothing but if I was not already knocked up, this nigga would probably have me with triplets or something!"

"Bitch, it's all good. I will be back trust and believe me, after the doctor's tomorrow."

Tiffany and Diamond were making final plans for tomorrow when Tree walked in. "Who are you on the phone with Tiff?

Tiffany answered smiling, "Diamond...we were joking around."

Tree was getting undressed, and had walked in the closet wearing only his boxers. Tiffany was wearing only her boy shorts and a wife beater. She got up from the bed and walked in the closet behind him.

"Where you going?"

"I got some loose end shit me and Von got to tie up."

She wrapped her arms around his waist and hugged him before circling around to the front of him. "So you got some loose ends and then what?"

While Tree was trying to talk, she slowly slid his boxers down and starting massaging his dick real slow.

"Tiff, stop playing, I got to go."

Still not listening to him, Tiffany slowly got down on her knees, took his balls in her hands and rubbed them gently.

"Tiff…oh shit…Tiff I got to go."

Tiffany begin licking on his balls real slow and blowing on them. Tree knew he had lost the battle and decided to give in. When he stop resisting she licked up his rock hard dick till she got to the tip of it, slowly pulled him into her mouth and held him there for a few minutes. She heard Tree moan out in ecstasy and started moving slow back and forth on his dick, pulling it almost out of her mouth, stopping at the tip and then taking the whole thing back in. He placed his hands on the back of her head and gently guided her in and out and each time she took him in a little deeper. When she was sure her pussy was nice and wet, she stood up, turned around, bent down in front of Tree and backed up onto his dick. Tree had been enjoying sex with Tiffany since the first time they had it, but since she had been pregnant her pussy was even better, fatter and wetter than usual. Tree grabbed a hold of Tiffany's hips and pulled her in till he hit bottom. He had a slight curve in his dick that made sex with him even better. Tiffany was now moaning as he glided in and out of her so slow that every time he would pull his dick just slightly from exiting her, he would hit her spot. She got louder, wanting Tree to fuck her harder. He reached over and shut the closet door hoping that

Tiffany's mother wouldn't hear them. He lifted Tiffany's wife beater over her head, massaged her breast and pinched her nipples real soft. Tiffany felt herself about to cum and backed up just a little more. Tree circled around in her pussy until he felt her G spot. Once he was there, he tapped on it until he felt her warm juices flow down his dick. He gave a slight laugh, turned Tiffany around and lifted her up onto his dick. He kissed her with passion and force as he moved in and out of her slowly. Tiffany felt his dick pulsating and hitting her walls. She used his shoulders to lift herself up and down moving faster on his dick. Tree helped her, still trying not to bust just yet.

"Ma, I want you to come with me."

Tiffany shook her head.

He bent down, licked her breast again, and repositioned her till he felt her spot.

"You ready baby?"

Again Tiffany shook her head.

Tiffany and Tree went at it like animals in heat. Tree made sure to back Tiffany up against the wall so he would not drop her when he got his nut. Tiffany started trembling and Tree knew it was time. She bit down on her bottom lip and they both came at the same time. Tree came so hard he opened his eyes slightly to make sure he had not shot her off his dick. He was enjoying his nut too much to even let her down. She leaned forward and rested her head on his chest.

Just as they were catching their breath, Tiffany's mother was knocking on the door. Tiffany and Tree were still in the closet. They laughed, and figured if they were quiet, she would assume they were sleep and go away.

When she stopped knocking, Tree let Tiffany down and they both went to the shower. While they were in the shower,

Tiffany asked Tree, "What do you have to do with Von? I thought that once you two handed your territory to Ish, you were both done.

Tree responded, "Even though we handed it over, there are still people we have to meet with and introduce Ish.

Tiffany had a bad feeling about that but decided to shake it off. "Well tomorrow, Diamond asked me to go to the doctor with her. Do you think I can get a pass for the day?"

"Are they going to pick you up?"

"Tree stop it, you're acting like I'm the one the doctor put on bed rest."

Tree looked at her like she was crazy and said, Baby, I know you have selective memory, but you are the one she told to be easy while you're pregnant."

"Yeah, but babe, she did not say I was high risk. She just to be easy and I've been good. Come on, please?"

Tree liked to hear her beg. "Let me think about it and I'll let you know, especially since you worked overtime just a few minutes ago."

Tiffany laughed and hit him. "Yeah, but that's good for the body. It's like milk…it does my body good!"

Tree exited the shower on that one and Tiffany followed right behind him. Tiffany was tired as hell now. She walked in the closet, got dressed in a Gucci fleece jumpsuit, and laid across the bed. Tree put on his all white Armani sneakers, Versace jeans and a crisp white Lacosta polo, kissed Tiff on the cheek and left.

Chapter TWENTY-ONE

Nina had been in VA for a couple of weeks now, recouping from her injuries and getting up strength to walk after Tiffany had cut her knee. During surgery a plastic plate was implanted in Nina's knee because the cut had damaged some of the bone. Doctor's advised her that this was necessary to avoid risk of infection. During recuperation, she reminisced about the last couple of years and how she had been living her life. All that time, she had used people and even stooped so low as to kill her own sister and steal her baby. She could not believe herself. How could one person be so ruthless and evil? She realized then that the main source of her anger was a man and a woman coming between her and a man. Why hadn't Ish dropped some hints to her before now? She could have dealt with waiting and being patient if he had just let her in on the plan. Ish had not been to see her in two days, but they talked everyday when he had down time. Nina was lonely as hell in VA, but she knew it was best because she had no one else to turn to—no family and no friends she could trust. Honestly, most of her friends were only there for the free ride and to help her spend Tree's money when he was good to her. So she sure couldn't call any of those tricks. Plus, word would get out that she was alive in VA and Ish had already told her word was on the street to pay anyone that could provide information on her whereabouts.

Nina was still worried about how Ish's plan was going to work out without getting both of them killed. Because even if Tree and Von were out of the game, the streets would forever be loyal to them for all the work they had given to the streets and the people they helped, especially their workers. And let's not forget their father who was a powerful man with half of Maryland's police and politicians on his payroll. But Ish assured her that he had been hashing out this plan for a long time and he had recruited his people from New York to help him on this one. He wanted Tree, Cito and Von dead and if need be, their wives too, and he planned on getting his way. He would be the king when it was over. He did not want just Tree and Von's territory, he wanted it all. The ultimate was Cito's position. Nina just thought it best she remain where she was. In her heart she did not see how Ish was really going to make it out of this shit alive.

Von and Tree sat in Von's Cadillac STS smoking a blunt. Tree seemed aloof, and just stared out the window, thinking.

"Yo, check it Von. I know I made the decision to put Ish in charge and we told our wives we was getting out this shit, and I plan on keeping my word, but something ain't sitting well at all."

Von was surprised at Tree's comments, but figured it was best to let the nigga speak his mind and get all the shit off his chest. The last couple of times he had met with Tree he had been real quiet, especially when Ish was around.

"Look Von, I was going to let you in on my thoughts, but

I figured I needed to be sure before I got you and Cito in the loop. And before you say it nigga, this ain't on no trust shit. You're my brother and Cito is like our father, but I know the two of y'all got short fuses and would have killed the nigga without question, just on suspicion. So I needed to do my homework. Plus I needed time to tell Tiff that Lil Mike will be the prince of this empire. Hell, as far as she knows the nigga is strictly geeked on the restaurant. She has no idea that he has been working with us and learning everything. Trust and believe, she and Diamond are going to flip when they find out, but that is beside the point.

Check it, I've been following this nigga Ish for a couple weeks now especially since word is out that Nina is alive and our instructions were for him to kill both of them before setting the car on fire. In addition, who the hell would have been going pass the dump sight at that time of the night to save her?"

By now, Von was looking at Tree like he had three heads because he really had kept a lot of shit from him, like how he knew for sure the bitch was alive.

Tree turned to face Von and said, "You remember that shorty I use to fuck here and there that works at Regional? Well, she was Nina's nurse. She called me, not knowing me and Nina were not together anymore and said they had brought her in a few hours earlier and she was in ICU. Well it struck me as weird the bitch survived, so I told her I would be up there but not to let anyone else know she was there. I didn't go that night but received a call from the chick again asking why I sent Ish there instead of checking on my girl myself. I told her Nina and I were not together so it was best Ish went up to check on her just in case she ain't want me to know she was in the hospital, since we're not an item. I told her again not to mention to anyone she talked to me, but just keep me updated on what's going on. She promised she would if I committed to come check her one day when she was off."

Von laughed a little, knowing Tree had already served her up. Not that he ain't love Tiffany, but business is business. Tree went on to tell Von that he got a call one day saying Nina had checked herself out of the hospital hours after Ish's visit, which confused her because Nina could barely walk. So I borrowed Lil Mike's car, sat across from the hospital, waited, and watched. Yo Von, Ish picked the bitch up, but this ain't the half of it. Now I think Ish has been stealing from us all this time. I don't know how because he was always square with his money when he turned it in."

This got Von's full attention and he asked him how he came to that conclusion.

"Well I followed them from the hospital. He took her to VA, pulled up to this phat-ass house that I know even with the good money Ish was making, he could not afford unless he was stealing from us. Think about it…he has the condo here, and two cars. Where would he get the money to afford a house like ours? Anyway, he's got Nina cooped up in that house. I was about to leave when I saw Ish coming out of the house, so I decided to see what else this snake was up to. Von, listen to me nigga and do this on the strength of our brotherhood, don't move on this nigga, not right now. Even though I know you're going to be heated, you've got a baby on the way, shit is hot, and if we move we will be going to death row."

Von took a hit off his blunt and said, "If shit is this bad maybe we need to call Cito, pick him up, talk about it, and get it out in the open one good time." Tree thought about it and agreed. Von chirped Cito's phone. Something they rarely used, so when it was used everyone knew it was important. Cito was relaxing at home when he heard the chirp and knew it was some shit, but prayed nothing was wrong with his boys.

"Yo!!"

"Yo, Cito, it's Von. Are you dressed?"

"I am laying down boy, it's 12:30 AM. What the fuck is up? Something wrong with your brother?" Cito held his breath waiting for a response.

"No man, nothing's wrong with Tree, he's right here. But check it, I need to come scoop you up, we need to talk."

Cito said he would be ready when they got there. Tree was deep in thought knowing Cito was going to snap because he held this information so long. They picked him up, drove down to the construction site and parked by the water edge. Cito finally spoke and asked why they couldn't have the conversation in the house. Tree told his father everything he told Von and other information that answered why they couldn't meet at the house.

"Look, we're all hot right now. Von and I are supposed to be getting out, but looks like it ain't going to be easy. As I was saying, when Ish left VA I followed his ass again. Well long story short, I saw him pull up to Agent Oarlock's house. He was in there a good four hours. When he came out they were shaking hands."

Cito was getting more pissed by the minute. He had paid all these motherfucker's a lot of money and they were trying to turn on him. Hell no, shit was about to get worse real quick…a war in the streets was getting ready to happen, and the outcome would be a lot of dead bodies.

Cito turned to Tree and asked, "Why'd you hold onto this

information. I feel betrayed."

Tree held his head in his hands and did his best to explain. "Look, like I told Von, y'all are my blood, even though there is none really between us flowing through our veins. I would never let any harm come to y'all, but I needed to make sure this nigga was really dirty because I know you and Von. Plus, I needed to see how many other players are in this game, so I can bring you all you needed to know, not no half-ass shit. This shit is bigger than Ish. There are some more players that need to go down."

Von smiled because he knew his brother meant no harm and he and Cito knew too that Tree meant no harm to La Familia.

Cito said, "Boy, I know you meant well, but La Familia helps one another. You're trying to carry all this shit on your shoulders but we're here. If you had told us, like you did now, not to jump on it, just watch, we would have done it."

Tree looked at both of them and they all burst out in laughter.

"Well, we would have tried."

Tree said, "Exactly, that's why I waited. Bottom line y'all, this nigga has been wired and they're trying to take us down for life. I guess just having my territory was not good enough, he wanted it all."

Von asked, "Did you know this before you signed your territory over to him?"

Tree shook his head no, and told Cito he was sorry.

Cito held his hand up and said, "Ish has been in La Familia for a long time. I am not sure why he turned on us, but he will be dealt with. Anyway, I want business to continue as usual, but I want you boys to have no hands on. If the nigga calls you, don't talk business on the phone. If you meet with him let him do all the talking, if you have to answer a question, use your heads, never speak answers. I will have Monty follow him, get pictures and info on all the people in this with him. They talked a little while longer and ended their meeting.

Chapter TWENTY-TWO

Ish had been feeling himself the last couple of weeks since gaining his territory. He was partying every night, and being very reckless about paying attention to his surroundings. Had he been like he was before he became, as he said, "the king". He would have noticed how Evan seemed to always be where he was or watching him. He would have also noticed when he was being followed on his trips back and forth to VA. Ish was loving spending so much time with Nina, constantly pressing her about having a baby. Nina was loving the idea and all the attention Ish was giving her and it did not hurt that she had free range of money whenever she wanted it. But Nina knew that the shit Ish was doing was bound to come to a haunt him. She also remembered being ditched on the curb by Tree with no money or anything, so little by little she would put away money that Ish was giving her, just in case shit went sour and she needed to get away fast.

On this particular night, Nina decided it was time for her and Ish to have a talk. "Ish can I ask you a question?"

"Sure what's on your mind, because whatever it is you

know I will fix it.?"

"Ish, what happens if this shit you're planning on pulling off backfires? We are finally with each other, and shit is going good, but what if that cop you're dealing with is really playing you, and he's on Cito's roll and they're all setting you up?"

"What the fuck, Nina, you still thinking about that nigga that did you dirty? You're worried about what's going to happen to him when I make them rain down on his ass and put him out of business for life?"

Ish got out of the bed and got dressed.

"You know that is not what I'm trying to say. All I'm saying is you've been living large. Why can't we just pick up, move south, and start over there where no one knows shit about us and who we are. If you're good enough to be king here, you're good enough to be king anywhere."

"Fuck that, Nina, I am not about to run like no bitch. This shit is all mine and I've planned this out for a while. Ain't nothing bad gonna happen to me, but Tree, his so-called brother, and his precious, untouchable, father, are going to feel my raft. Look, I don't want to talk about this shit no more, I'm out. When you get your mind right, check for your boy."

Nina jumped up and ran toward the door begging Ish not to leave, but he was pissed. He pushed her to the side and left.

When he got back to Maryland, he went straight to Breakers to get his drink on and floss a little of his street money. He was having a good time and the bitches were all over him half the night. One particular girl had his full, undivided attention. She was beautiful as hell, and he had been watching her on the dance floor throughout the night. Ish left the chick that was in his face and walked out of VIP. He stood over to the side near the dance floor watching this woman that looked to be Black and Hawaiian. As she was winding slowly on the dance floor by herself, he looked her over from head to toe, and she was screaming money and sophistication all over. He walked up to her from behind, pulled her slightly close to him to dance with her. When the song was over Ish took her by the hand and led her back to VIP. The chick that was in his face earlier was still waiting and now had her face twisted up. He told her to get up.

"Ish, you said we were going to chill tonight. Why you bring this skeeza up here?"

Ish looked over to Larry, his go getter man, who walked over, snatched the girl out of the booth and removed her completely from VIP. Ish sat down and pulled the beautiful women in the booth with him. He looked at her for a long time with approval. She was even more beautiful in the light than he had imagined her on the dance floor.

"So what is your name?"

"Autumn, and yours?"

"Mine name is Ishmael, but everyone calls me Ish. So, where is your man?"

Autumn laughed and asked, "Why do I have to have a man? Why can't I just be doing Autumn?"

"You're too pretty just to be doing you and by the looks of things, someone is taking good care of you and that body of yours and milk ain't the only one, so what's up?"

"To be honest with you Ishmael, I don't have a man. I just moved here from Houston. I'm a student and I do some modeling. I tend to keep to myself and men don't really try to holler because, like you, they assume I have a man or that I'm uppity and they don't want to play themselves. And that's fine by me because Autumn makes her own money and just does her."

Ish liked her answer a lot. "So Miss Independent Autumn, who are you here with?"

She laughed and said, "I guess you don't hear well or maybe I just didn't make myself clear,…I just do me. I have maybe five girlfriends that I trust with my life and maybe two here that I associate with. But most times since I've been in Maryland, I just kind of do me, by myself, for myself. You feel me Ishmael?"

Ish was loving how she said his name and loved her southern accent. "Well yeah, I feel you and I must say, I like your style and want to get to know you better. Unlike the boys that have been walking around scared to holler at you, I am a man. I am single and I can hold me down and you too, for that matter. So can I get your number and maybe swing by tomorrow, scoop you up and we do some shopping and lunch or dinner?"

Autumn thought for a minute and said, "Hey, it can't hurt. I'm sure I can fit you in my budget and buy you a shirt or two."

Ish laughed and said, "No baby, you save your money. Tomorrow is strictly on your boy."

Ish and Autumn chilled, drank some more and even got a few more dances in before calling it a night.

* * *

"Hey Von, it's me Autumn, what it do?"

"Shit girl, how did it go at the club last night, did that nigga show the fuck up?"

"Yeah, of course, his corny ass was there and like y'all said…he bit the bullet. Not to mention, I am a bad bitch."

Von laughed. "At times you can be but that's beside the

point. Anyway, your apartment is hooked up and finished, your pictures are up on canvas like you requested and you straight as far as everything else goes. When you get your lazy ass together, your key and address is downstairs at the hotel's front desk. Did the nigga follow you home?"

"No and stop asking me stupid questions like I'm new to this shit. I do me, you know that. Y'all want me to set the nigga up nice, and you're paying me good...I got you. Matter of fact, Von, hold on, that clown is calling right now and to think I ain't even give him no dirty-south head or pussy yet and he's sniffing hard and wanting to take me shopping."

Autumn clicked over and Von busted out laughing. When she clicked back over she said, "Von, it's been nice talking to you, but I got to get out of bed, get dressed and to the apartment within the next two hours so this nigga can pick me up and I can do some damage to his pockets. Oh, tell Diamond I need her to cook me a good, southern, Sunday dinner tomorrow because even a trick needs a home cooked meal while working away from home." Autumn laughed and hung up on Von before he could say anything else.

Von called Tree and gave him the run down. Tree was pleased because he knew with Autumn on the job, shit was going to go smooth. She would get this nigga talking like a humming bird, and when it was all over she would rock his ass to sleep for being disloyal.

Chapter TWENTY-THREE

Autumn had been down with Tree and Von for many years. She was a young, hot-head back in the day, and had tried to rob Von back when he first stared working the corners. Von whipped her ass good that night, giving her something to remember him by the next time she thought about trying to stick him up. The next day, Von went looking for her and found her at her mother's apartment in filth.

"Yo, young thugget, where your people at?"

"Fuck you, you're going to whip my ass then come up in here, all in my business."

Von smiled because she was trying hard to be like the thug-ass dudes from the street. He walked around the apartment and saw there were no lights, no food anywhere in sight, nor any furniture, well none you could consider furniture. Von went back toward the front of the house, pulled Autumn up by her hand, and told her to come on.

"I ain't going no place with you nigga. What you want, some pussy? Well, it's going to cost you like it cost all those other mother fuckers that sniff around here."

Von slapped her in her mouth, and told her, "The next time I am going to rock your ass into a nap. Now I told you to bring your ass on."

In shock, she followed Von and got in his car. Autumn had never been in an Acura so she was enjoying the ride. Von pulled up to the mall and got out. Autumn slowly got out and stood by the car.

"Look Von, I ain't about to go in here and apply for no job, so you can go ahead and slap me or whatever, right now. Plus, I don't know what makes you think you can work the streets and I can't. I know what you do, so don't be trying to play goody-goody with me."

Von walked off, leaving her near the car in the heat. Seeing Von walk into the mall and as hot as it was, she decided to follow because one, she had no money for a bus, and two, it was too far to walk back around the way. She would just go in, fill out the freaking applications to make him feel like he'd done a good deed, and go back to the block.

Autumn finally caught up with Von and walked beside him but kept her mouth shut. The first store they went into was Sax Fifth Ave. Von called over a young saleslady and asked her to pull out all the hot shit they had in Autumn's size and any matching shoes. He took a seat on the couch in the dressing area and placed a call, not saying another word to Autumn or the saleslady. The saleslady went to work and called the shoe department to bring up all the hot new shoes that came in.

She whispered in the phone, "There's a high roller and his sister in the store."

Autumn looked at her and rolled her eyes because she overheard her comments. The saleslady took Autumn in the dressing room with all the clothes she had pulled for her, and the salesman from the shoe department came running toward the dressing room with a cart full of shoes. The saleslady came out to get a couple more things and Von stopped her.

"Yo, when you get a chance, call and set a hair appointment for her." Von handed her a $50 tip and went back to his phone conversation.

After a whole day of being made over, Autumn was at a loss of words. "So Von, what I owe you for all this?"

Von looked at her, smiled and said, "What you owe me is for you to get your shit together and find another hustle. But don't worry about that now, all you got to do right now is promise me that if you're down with me, you're down with me for life and you will forever be loyal to La Familia."

Autumn had never known what it was like to be part of a family, but had always wished she had one. She was honest with Von and told him just that and promised she would never turn on the one person that even after she did him dirty, still stuck his neck out for her. Autumn told Von she owed her life to him for making her feel special, if only for a day. Von said your life is yours, just always promise loyalty. That Autumn promised and meant what she said.

They pulled up to a two story house and Autumn looked at Von with questions written all over her face.

"Autumn where are your people?"

Autumn lowered her head. "I don't have a clue. They come and go as they please and that's why I'm in the streets taking care of myself."

Von got out of the car and proceeded up the stairs. Autumn thought to herself, *here we go with this walk off shit, he just has no manners at all.* She got out and followed him into the apartment. When they walked in, all she could smell was food and her stomach started making noise because she had not eaten in almost twenty-four hours. Diamond came out the kitchen and greeted Von with a kiss.

Diamond looked Autumn over and said, "Hi Autumn, I'm Diamond, Von's wife."

"Nice to meet you," Autumn said.

"Y'all have a nice place." Diamond laughed and said we probably do, but this is your place. I just came to stock the refrigerator and figured I would fix you something to eat, because I knew after hanging with grumpy over there you would be hungry.

Autumn looked at Diamond like she was crazy and then at Von.

"I guess he has not said much of anything to you today, huh?"

"No, I have just been following him like a little puppy dog."

Diamond laughed. "Well after you tried to rob him, he came home mad but at the same time, you struck an interest in him. When y'all were at the mall he called and told me that he was 'adopting you, end of discussion'." Diamond went on to tell Autumn that Von is not really one to show emotions or speak a lot unless he is talking to her or his brother, and he has never taken a interest in anyone, so she should feel honored.

Autumn pulled Diamond back toward the kitchen and whispered to her. "I just want to thank you two for everything and I will never disappoint you."

Diamond hugged her and said, "I know you won't. Anyway Autumn, I have to get him home so I can feed him, but I will be here tomorrow at 10:00 to pick you up to register for school and I will be taking you to go get a car."

Autumn said, "Car and school?"

"Yes, you will go to school and if you don't agree, say something now and we will gladly take you back where you came from. There will be no fools up in this family. And the car is so you can get to class and wherever else you need to go. One last thing Autumn, we have girls hair day and the La Familia meets every Thursday, so make no plans for Thursdays. I stocked your drawer with all the necessary things from Victoria Secret you should need but of course, if I missed anything, let me know. Your bathroom is stocked well and you have all the pots, pans, towels and anything else you might need. Von should have your clothes up here by now, so you are straight on that. And, oh, one last thing, don't bring any and everyone up in your place. This is yours, other people ain't going to respect your shit like you do, and a nigga with nothing will surely try to take advantage of you if he feels he can dick you and then you take care of him."

Autumn was overwhelmed with all of the day's events. Diamond hugged her, picked up her Prada and said her good nights. Von nodded his head at Autumn and followed behind Diamond. That day had changed Autumn's life and she was forever loyal to La Familia. She soaked in everything that Von, Tree and Diamond taught her about the game and the streets. None of Von and Tree's street soldiers had met Autumn because after she graduated high school, Von sent her off to Dallas to further her education and at the same time make a name for the La Familia down there. Of course, Tree was back and forth watching her so that made everyone comfortable with her being so far from home.

Chapter TWENTY-FOUR

Tiffany could not believe her ears when Tree put her down on everything that was going on. As she listened to what Ish was trying to pull she began to get sick just thinking about the possibility that Tree could be taken from her by either the Feds or the streets. And, what about their baby? She became nauseous, jumped up and ran for the bathroom to throw up. Tree ran in behind her and wet a cloth to cool her forehead.

"Tiff you OK?"

"Hell no, I ain't OK. What the fuck? This is unreal. You're out the game, gave this nigga everything, and he pulled this right here? And then you tell me that bitch, Nina, is still alive and y'all still letting her walk after what she did to my cousin? No! Hell no! I might be pregnant, but this shit y'all talking about, waiting and being patient, is bullshit and I ain't trying to hear none of it. Tree, you need to tell me where Nina is so I can dead her myself since it is evident that she was not taken care of before. Let me ask you this while we're on the subject…you got feelings or something for her? Why you know where she is and she still living? Get your fucking hands off me and move out my way Tree, because right now I want to jump on your ass."

Tree looked at her and if it had not been for her carrying his baby, he might have slapped her because that is how mad she had made him. "Yo, you need to fall back and watch how you talking Tiff because you're getting real greasy with me right now. You know good and fucking well ain't shit being felt over here about Nina on my part. Second, deading her right now, after what I just told you…how the fuck it look Tiff, huh? You're the one with the big time fucking education, answer that one for me scholar, how it look? I just told your selfish ass that Ish got us hot right now and they're watching our every move. Shit, on the way home I had a fucking car follow me all the way in and we all know ain't no cars coming down in the country from the city following me to a tee."

Tiffany knew she had crossed the line and knew he was pissed as hell. She sat on the edge of the bed holding her head in her hands and began to cry. "Tree, I'm sorry. My emotions are just all over the place and I'm scared." She stood up and walked toward Tree but when she reached out to touch him, he stepped back. He stared at her for a long time, turned and walked out of the room. Tiffany went behind him trying to make it right, but he walked out of the house, got in his car and pulled out of the driveway.

Tiffany called Diamond to tell her what just went down. Diamond asked, "Have you lost your fucking mind? What's really going on with you?"

Tiffany began to cry again. "I don't know I'm just real emotional and moody at the same time."

"You need to calm down because you are in her eighth month and stress was not going to make things any better."

Diamond had her baby a month before they found out Ish was a traitor. She was happy she had their daughter, Kenyetta McKnight, before all this or she would have definitely gone into labor after she heard about it.

"I'll call you back. I'm going to try and reach Tree on his cell." She called several times but he never answered her call.

Tree was hot with Tiffany but, hell, he had been getting the same question from everyone about why he held the info and why these people were still walking around. He knew he was right by holding onto the information till he put all the pieces together. Plus he knew that if he told, bodies would start showing up in the streets and with the Feds watching them, they would have surely been caught in the act and serving life. No, he was right in what he did, he was protecting La Familia.

Tree sat outside of the strip club for hours thinking and planning out some things in his head. He was not in the mood to see anyone but he had no place else to go. He was not ready to deal with members of La Familia right now with all their questions and opinions. The car that had been following him sat in the cut and he sure hoped they didn't think they were dealing with fools and knew that every member of La Familia was not as dumb as Ish. Tree sipped his drink, hit his blunt and continued to think. When Tree was all thought out and tipsy he started his car and waited for the car that had been tailing him to start up. Tree laughed and thought, at *least I know I have someone to follow me home to make sure I make it safe*. With that he peeled out the driveway and headed home. He slept on the couch that night but went up to check on Tiffany before going to sleep. When he peeked in their room she was curled up on top of the comforter, still in her sweat suit with the phone in her hand. He covered her up, took the phone out of her hand and went back downstairs. Tree could not wait until morning because he had the best fool proof plan possible to share with Cito and Von.

Tiffany woke up and noticed that Tree was not next to her. She was upset with herself for upsetting Tree and accusing him of still having feelings for Nina. She jumped up when she felt she was about to throw up and ran for the bathroom. She sure wished these nine months would be over so she could get her body back, meet her baby and at times like this, take a drink. She was sitting on the floor when she felt something warm and wet between her thighs. She stuck her hand between her legs and knew she was either pissing on herself or her water had broken. She panicked and crawled to the phone, just then a sharp pain shot through her feeling like it went from her back to her stomach and back again. She cried out in pain. "Why now while I am home alone?" She picked up the phone trembling and hit the speed dial for Tree. While his phone was ringing another pain shot through her and she thought she was going to pass out. These pains were like nothing she ever felt before in her life. Tree heard her scream through the house before he could say hello into the phone. He jumped up, ran up the stairs two at a time and found Tiffany balled up in a fetal position on the floor.

"Tiff, what the fuck? What's wrong?"

Tiffany screamed, "My water broke…I'm in labor!"

Tree got excited. "OK, let me call Diamond."

"Diamond? You need to call the doctor, EMS, or something."

Tree called the doctor first and told him they were on their way to the hospital. Next, he hit Von on the Nextel. Von told Tree they would meet them at the hospital and ended the conversation.

Tree lifted her off the floor and got her in the car. As soon as they pulled off, Tiffany screamed again.

"Look lil momma, you're going to have to stop screaming before you cause us to have an accident."

Tiffany shot him a look that said if I could I would slap you but the baby must have sensed her thoughts and decided to hit her with another one. Tiffany clamped her teeth tight and said, "When this is over you owe me and I will not be doing this ever again!"

Tree kept trying to rub her stomach but she kept pushing his hand away. When they pulled up to the hospital, Tree let out a slight laugh. Standing outside waiting was Diamond with what looked like 100 balloons. Tree jumped out, picked Tiffany up and took her into the hospital. Diamond stayed with her while he moved the car. Once they had her in a room and hooked up to monitors things seem to move very fast. The doctor came in smiling but Tiffany found nothing to smile about, and wanted to line everyone in the room up and slap all of them. There were still three more weeks before she was due but like father, like child, the baby had plans of its own.

After two hours, Tiffany gave birth to a beautiful baby girl. Kennedy Nicole was six pounds-two ounces. Kennedy had slanted eyes like her father and a head full of black hair. Tree could not stop staring at her and refused to let her out of his sight. Diamond stayed with her cousin while Von and Tree followed the nurse and Kennedy to the nursery to clean her up before bringing her back to Tiffany's room.

Diamond said, "With the girls being only months apart, I hope they grow up to be as tight as we are."

Tiffany smiled in agreement, leaned on her for a long hug

and drifted off to sleep. Von and Diamond left after a couple of hours at the hospital. Tree pulled the baby's basinet close to his chair and drifted off to sleep.

Tiffany woke first and to her surprise, Ish was standing at the door with flowers and a box from Gucci. She was stunned but tried to keep a straight face.

"Hey Ish, what's up?"

"Oh man, congrats. You know I heard the word you had the baby, so I wanted to come show my face and congratulate y'all."

Tiffany called Tree a couple of times before he finally woke up. Seeing Ish standing there made Tree's blood boil, but he tried to contain himself. "Yo, what's up, what you doing here?"

"I heard that Tiff had the baby and you know I had to show fam some love."

Tree repeated the word *fam* to himself and said, "Well, I appreciate it, but who knew on the street that fast?"

"Oh man, you know word gets out. Someone must have seen y'all come in or something. I was on the block collecting money and word on the street was Tree's wife had the baby today. So I ran up to see what was up."

Tree knew the nigga was lying and that the only way he knew was from the fed motherfuckers who had been following him. "Well thanks for stopping by Ish, you know we're just doing the family thing right now."

"Oh man, I can feel that. I just want to take a peek at the little one."

Ish looked in the basinet, smiled and complimented, "Y'all did good, son. Well let me get out of here."

Tree was ready to blow this nigga's brains out because he knew he was trying to make a joke by smiling on his baby like he was running some shit and he held the world in his hands. Tree knew he had to number this cat's days because he was getting too cocky for his own good and on top of that, he had lied and been disloyal. Tree decided to play the devil himself a little.

"So Ish, where you been hiding? The streets say you got some fine tender you flossing."

Ish smiled hard and said, "Yeah, her name is Autumn and she's bad."

Tiffany heard Autumn's name and almost choked on her water. Ish asked if she was OK and she responded, "Yes, my throat is dry, pardon me."

"OK, but yeah, man this chick so bad that I might have to wife her, but we'll see. She's a model, goes to college, and of course you always need one with a good head on her shoulders."

"Well I'm happy to hear it. Sounds like you're feeling her."

"Man yeah, matter fact, I got to run because I'm supposed to scoop her from class. So I will check y'all later."

Ish left and Tiffany looked at Tree for answers. He shook his head and said, "I'll tell you about it later when we're home. Tiffany didn't push it.

Chapter TWENTY-FIVE

Cito was excited when he got word he was a grandfather again. He called Tree when he hung up from Von.

Tree answered, "Well granddad, once again, what it do?"

Cito laughed. "You tell me."

Tree put Cito on hold to connect Von on a three-way. When they connected, Tree told them about the hospital visit from Ish. Cito put them on hold made a call and told his workers to get to the hospital like yesterday to move Tiffany out of the hospital now. He gave them instructions to make sure they are not seen, nor is she and the baby. He instructed one of them to exchange clothes with Tree, drive off in his car, and have the Feds follow him. Once y'all are sure that the Feds are on you and not the car with the baby and Tiffany, let them know they've followed the wrong person. Cito got back on the phone and told Tree what was getting ready to happen.

Von heard a knock on his door. "Hold on so I can answer this."

Cito responded, "No need. Get off the phone and do what

you are instructed." He ended the conversation.

Nina had not seen Ish in about two weeks and when she spoke to him he was short and brief like he could not be bothered. She was not sure what was going on but she damn sure was going to find out. She bought a wig, rented a car, drove to Maryland and staked out across the street from Ish's condo. She had been there for about two hours and was getting tired of waiting. Just when she was about to start her car, she saw Ish come out with some exotic looking chick. Her mouth fell open and all she could say was, "What the fuck?"

Ish walked the girl to her car holding her hand, leaned her against the car and kissed her like his life depended on it. Nina began to cry because yet another motherfucker had played her. Here she thought he was real when he told her he was there for her, would not hurt her because he had always loved her, and now he is damn near fucking some girl in front of his house. She wanted to walk up to him and shoot his ass but decided that revenge was the best way and what better way to get at him than rat his ass out to La Familia who he was suppose to be loyal to.

Cito sat in the Jacuzzi with Sunshine. Sunshine had always been his favorite when he wanted to relieve a little stress. They met at his Panama home one weekend when he was tying up loose ends with a new client he had been introduced to by his nephew. Sunshine was hired help that served them throughout their stay at the villa. Cito always requested model-like chicks and they were not allowed to wear anything but a bikini. Panama had a lot of cuties, but Sunshine just held Cito's eyes with her olive complexion, long honey-brown hair, and hazel eyes. She also had a size 36DD breast, and the longest, sexiest legs any man would love wrapped around him. Sunshine spoke very little but always made sure Cito was taken care of both during his business meetings and in the bedroom. She loved older men and the first time she worked for Cito she knew that he would be hers whenever he was there or when he sent for her to be with him.

Sunshine could sense that something was wrong…one, because he sent for her and two, because he had not said much and had not been all over her like usual. She usually did not ask questions about his business but she had been in town for a week and he made love to her on a regular while she was there, but not like he usually did when they had their play weekends. "Cito, you know I don't get in your business and I know my place with you, but I have been here for a week and I can tell something is bothering you. Is there something I can do to help you?"

Sunshine began to massage his manhood and could feel him rising as she stroked him up. Cito pulled her closer to him and lifted her up to come down on him. He stared in her eyes while they sat in the Jacuzzi and she grinded slowly on his dick.

"I never involve outsiders in my business and I will be OK. I just learned that no one can truly be trusted and I'm faced with being setup and will not go down without a fight. I will die before I give the government any of my time."

Sunshine continued to work her magic as thoughts ran through her head. She could not lose Cito over bullshit. He had been good to her and what little he asked in return, she didn't mind doing. Sunshine lifted herself off of Cito's swollen manhood, went under the water and began sucking his dick. Cito, for a minute, forgot all about his troubles as Sunshine took him to another place. He didn't want to come in his Jacuzzi, so he lifted her out, turned her around quickly, and hit it from the back with such force that he was sure he was hurting her but didn't care. He just needed to release his stress. Cito busted so hard he thought he had busted a hole in his own dick or hit her in the throat with it through her pussy. He laughed at that thought as he pulled out from Sunshine and relaxed for a moment before going into the house. Sunshine decided she would hang around awhile longer to find out just what was going on and put an end to the shit, if she had to start deading niggas herself. Especially since in her mind she just knew she and Cito had made a baby that night.

Chapter TWENTY-SIX

Agent Oarlock could not have been happier to finally get someone that was willing to help him take Cito and his faggot-ass sons down. It made agent Oarlock's dick hard just thinking about looking in Cito's face when they went to arrest him and put his ass away for life. For five years, he had been trying to get someone to roll on Cito but either people were too afraid or they were being paid so well they would not dare roll on him or his sons. Agent Oarlock grew up in the neighborhood with Cito and tried many times to be his partner when Cito was on the come-up, but Cito was stingy and wanted no partners. He felt that sharing his crown was out of the question. The thing that made Oarlock vow to bring Cito down was when he walked in on his fiancé being fucked by Cito, who looked back at him and winked as he continued to dig her out doggy-style. Oarlock loved that woman, and worked two jobs to give her everything. When he confronted her all she would say was Cito could offer her the world and fuck her whenever she needed the dick. Years later, Oarlock was able to laugh in her face when he ran across her during a raid on a crack house where she was so deep in a nod she didn't even know the raid was going on. She was high off of the glass dick. Oarlock made sure once she sobered up in lockup, he was one of the first faces she saw. He grinned at her and said, "Cito's world seems not to agree with you," and walked away. Oarlock had been through two marriages and blamed their failing on Cito and Rhonda. Now with Ish in his corner and working for the Feds, he needed just this takedown to laugh in Cito's face to complete the payback. Cito and Oarlock ran into each other a few times when Oarlock had bagged Cito's sons on some bullshit charges. Both Von and Tree served two years for the shit but they served them laughing at Oarlock because what he thought would put them away forever was just a rest for them. As hard as the Feds tried to get Von and Tree to roll on Cito, they were not trying to hear it. Oarlock had been watching Sunshine and figured he could get to Cito through her if he threatened her with major mandatory fed time. He had been keeping a log of her coming in and out of Maryland from Panama and could beef up charges that she was trafficking drugs for Cito. Yeah, Brian Oarlock was ready for the come-up and payback at the same time.

"Ish, this is Oarlock. When can we meet and where?"

Ish was just waking from a long night with Autumn. He looked at the clock and said, "Man, I can meet you in VA in about an hour at Nina's house."

Little did Ish know Autumn was far from sleep.

"I've got to put in time with Nina anyway because you know I've been tied up with you, this bullshit and my new chick."

Oarlock, getting disgusted said, "Look Ish, I am not fucking around...fuck these hoes. You need to keep Nina as happy as possible right now because I will need that bitch at trial to testify on what she knows about Tree and Cito's involvement in this shit. I already have enough shit on her if we need it to get her to testify, but I ain't trying to pull that murder card on her if I don't have to. Do your fucking job Ish, and stay on these niggas till the bust. One more week, and we will be able to move in on them. When is the next shipment supposed to come in involving all of them before Tree and Von retire and move?"

Ish could not stand this nigga. He was always screaming at him about doing what he wanted. Ish was getting bitched by the Feds, all in an attempt to be the next man and who was to say they would not later come back and take him down?

"Look man, the drop is on Sunday night at the harbor warehouse. Anyway, have you thought about what I asked you about us partnering up after the heat dies down on this thing?"

Ish figured if he pretended that Oarlock was his partner that would keep him from under the radar of the Feds.

"Yeah, I thought about it, and I will be a silent partner once all this shit is over."

Ish was confused as to what the fuck that meant. "What you mean silent partner?"

"I mean I will get paid to make sure your back is covered and you do whatever you do."

Ish was pissed, because basically that meant Ish got his hands dirty and if any foul shit went down it was his word against Oarlock because no one but them would know that they were partners. Somehow Ish had to figure a way to take down Cito and Oarlock too. Autumn made a mental note to remember to have the shipment date cancelled to avoid the bust going down.

Autumn had been dating Ish now for four months and she was getting bored with pretending that he was the man. The sight of him made her sick knowing that he was the biggest bitch out there in the game. She was mad that Von and Tree were sitting on this nigga instead of letting her kill him herself and be done with this shit. It would have been one thing if his sex game was straight but he had no clue what to do with her and the pretending had gotten old quick. She could not wait for him to go see Nina so she could make a run over to Lil Mike's for some much needed back breaking sex.

Autumn and Lil Mike had been kicking it for the longest, although he was not deep in the game because Tiffany would kill them all for having her brother in the life. Autumn loved him anyway and she was happy he was not deep in the shit and was holding down the restaurant because the thought of him being locked up and away from her was out of the question. She pretended to be waking, so Ish could get his ass on and she could go and spend some time with her man. Lil Mike had been a trooper through this whole thing. He knew La Familia came first, knew her story and that she owed Von her life.

Ish got off the phone, rolled on top of Autumn and gave her a kiss. "Good morning love, how did you sleep? Did daddy put you to bed proper?"

Autumn smiled but inside she was thinking, *he can't be serious and to think bitches on the streets had been talking about how good he was in bed. What the fuck were they on when they fucked him, or was there another Ish that ran with La Familia?* "I slept very well. Thank you for the sleeping pill."

"What are you getting into today," Ish asked?

"I think I am going to catch up on some work and maybe

drive to DC to see my aunt." What about you?"

"Oh, I'm going to put in some work in these streets and collect some money. You know I have that big shipment coming in and I want to make sure all my people are ready to move this shit."

Autumn again was thinking, *if you only knew you ain't getting that shipment and your life span is getting shorter by the minute.* "Oh, OK. I feel that."

Autumn's phone vibrated letting her know she had a text message. She grabbed her iPhone, read the text from her baby and hit him back asking if they could go away for the weekend because she needed some quality time. Lil Mike instantly hit her back and told her he would be packed and waiting and for her to hurry up. Autumn rolled away from Ish and headed to the shower.

He followed behind her wanting to take a shower with her and hit that wet, hot pussy one more time before he had to go deal with Nina and her mouth about him not coming through in awhile. Autumn rolled her eyes at the fact that he had followed her and figured she would dead this real quick. She faced him, got on her knees, slowly pulled his boxers down as she made her way to the floor. She took his dick in her hands and massaged it slowly as she licked the tip of it. She knew he was a fast nutter so this would be the best way because he damn sure was not running up in her again right before she went to Mike to get what she really needed in her life. Autumn licked down the shaft of his dick to his balls, put one at a time in her mouth, then began to deep throat him several times really fast before playing with the tip of his dick with her tongue. After a couple of times of doing this, Ish warned her that he was about to cum. She rubbed his balls real slow and did one more deep throat move before she moved and he squirted all over the place. Autumn got up and got in the shower, leaving Ish trying to collect his thoughts.

Chapter TWENTY-SEVEN

Tiffany was enjoying having Tree home and out of the streets so much, but he was withdrawn and spent a lot of time holding the baby and staring into space. Tree had confided in her about everything that was going down and she was worried that the streets were finally catching up with him and he would be taken from her and their daughter. She wanted to help but didn't know what to do. She called her cousin to find out why she hadn't been calling and why they had not met to discuss what was going on. Diamond told her that she too had been stressed with the possibility of the Feds coming in and tearing up her family. Von also had been spending a lot of time at home, and that was so out of character for him too. Diamond told Tiffany that Von had recently confided in her that he would not be taken quietly and that they needed to prepare for the worse. If the best comes out of it good, but with Ish working with the Feds he didn't know what to do. Ish right now was untouchable because he was under fed watch and so were they.

After a long conversation, Diamond promised Tiffany she

would be to see her in a couple of days. Tree eavesdropped on their conversation from the doorway and startled her when she turned around.

"Why are you standing there?"

He responded, "I was just admiring your beauty.

Tiffany smiled, walked over to him and hugged him.

"Don't be mad at Diamond for not calling. I'm sure Von is still a little pissed at me for holding that info about Ish out on him until I knew for sure, and Diamond is just trying to keep the peace."

"Tree, so what is really going to happen now if y'all go through with this shipment on Sunday, and Ish knows about it?"

Tree shrugged his shoulders and said: "I knew what it was when I got in the game, and although I would never want to leave y'all, I have to hold my brother and father down by any means. We are just waiting on Cito to make the call."

Tiffany did not like that at all. "Well what about Nina? She knows a lot about the business and if they're together, even if you get Ish, she might be working with the Feds and be able to turn state's evidence on y'all for the sake of Ish."

Tree rubbed his hands over his head and said, "Tiff, I don't know, and I don't want to talk about it anymore." He grabbed her hand, led her to the bathroom and turned the water on in the Jacuzzi. Tiffany slowly undressed him, then herself, and slid into the Jacuzzi. When Tree was seated, Tiffany slid on top of him, looked into her husband's eyes.

She said softly, "I promise you, I will ride with you for life."

Tree wanted to believe he could ask her to hold him down on a life sentence. Shit was getting ready to get crazy and he just hoped that in the end he would still be standing. They made love in the Jacuzzi and then moved to the shower. He had so much pinned up stress and was happy that Tiffany wanted to help him anyway she could to release it. Tiffany knew the doctor told her six weeks and she had three to go, but she needed to be as close as possible to her husband right now and share that bond with him.

Tree lifted her on him and said, "Tiff, I want you to pack you and the baby and leave in the morning for your mother's and don't come back here till I call for you. And, even when I call you, go to Atlanta. Never come back to Maryland…this is no longer our home.

Tiffany thought Tree had lost his mind. "Hell no, I am not about to leave you here to deal with this shit alone. We are married and I'm not going anyplace without you."

It was killing Tree and breaking his heart but this shit was not up for discussion at all. He had made up his mind. "Look Tiff, this shit ain't up for debate, it is what it is. I am about to go to war and I will die if anyone tries to come at you. Your plane tickets are on the table in the dinning room and your bank account is straight, so you shouldn't need for anything. Evan drove your car down to Charlotte this morning and I've already talked to your mom."

Tiffany began to cry, not believing her ears. This could not be happening to her. She had just given him a baby, they were doing well, and now she was being forced to leave him when she knew he needed her the most. "Look Tree, I will take the baby and come back."

Tree did not want to have to pull his anger card on her because he wanted her to leave on a good note, but he knew she would not leave him at this point in his life. Tree lifted her off him, got out of bed and got dressed. Tiffany was confused, they were having a conversation, and now he was just deading it? *Hell no!*

"Tree where the fuck you think you're going and we're still talking?"

"Tiffany, look man, you talk all you want. I told you what the fuck is up, so stop running your mouth and just do what the fuck you're told. I got enough shit on my back and I don't need to hear your shit, or have you adding to my stress right now."

Tiffany jumped up and slapped Tree as hard as she could, out of anger and hurt. Tree drew back to slap her back but knew she was just hurt and he really had no intentions of hurting her, but he would die before he let harm come to his family. He turned to walk out and Tiffany kept landing blows to his back. Finally, Tree turned around and slammed her against the wall, grabbed her face, and stared in her eyes. He was hoping that she could read through his eyes and know that he would never want to let go of her. He let go of her face, pushed her on the bed and walked out the house. Tree had never really cried over anything but that just broke his heart. He could hear Tiffany screaming as he got into the car and wanted to run back and comfort her, but instead he headed to Cito's house in silence.

His cell phone rang and he recognized Autumn's number. "Yo, what's up?"

"Look, meet me at the restaurant." Autumn hung up.

Tree laughed, thinking she surely got that hang-up shit honest. He made a U-turn and headed for the restaurant.

He called Von. "Yo, Von, you talk to Autumn?"

"Naw. What's going on? My cell is in the car."

"Oh, OK, she wants us to meet her at the restaurant."

"Cool, I'll be there in ten." Tree wanted to ask if Von was sending Diamond away but figured that was not his business, it was that man's family.

Tiffany could feel knots in her stomach from what had just happen. How could Tree do this to her? She was ready to ride with him and he closed her out and sent her away like she was a jump-off and not his wife. Yeah, he explained his reasons but they had been dealing with things head-on together since they met. What she was not understanding was how he made love to her as he did, then be ready to kick her ass the next minute.

She pulled herself together when she heard the baby crying and went to comfort her, wondering where her comfort would come from. She needed her husband. She fed and quieted the baby, and tried calling Tree a couple of times. Finally giving up, she started packing and tried to reach Diamond, but got no answer. What was really going on? No one was answering her calls. She left messages for both and made herself comfortable on the couch to hear Tree when he came home. She fell asleep waiting but was awakened by the door bell around 4 AM. She hurried to the peephole to see who it was. The person ringing the bell was not visible. Tiffany went to the kitchen, grabbed her .32 and slowly opened the door finding a package on the doorstep. She looked around not seeing anyone, picked up the package and backed into the house. The package was addressed to her without a sender's name. She considered not opening it but thought it could be important. The contents of the box almost made her sick. It was a picture of Diamond and her daughter with pieces of their hair and a dead rose, painted black. She dropped the box and backed away from it. Rushing to the phone she first dialed Tree without answer, then called Von.

"Yo, Tree, Tiffany's calling me."

"Don't answer it man, she's just looking for me. Have

you decided if you are sending Diamond away till this is over or not?"

Von looked at Tree and said, "I tried but she ain't going no place. She's taking the baby to Charlotte and coming back. You know Diamond is a thug for life. She is cut from the same cloth as we are."

Tree laughed and proceeded to the back of the restaurant to meet with Autumn. Tiffany knew they had to be together because Von always answered her calls. She was thinking hard about who she should call…CITO!

Tiffany dialed Cito's number and a girl with an accent answered, "Hello."

"Yes, hello, may I speak to Cito?"

"No, you can not. Who is this?"

Tiffany didn't have time for tricks and games. "This is his daughter-in-law. And who the fuck are you, and why are you answering his phone?"

"Oh, I am sorry. This is Sunshine, please hold and, again, I am so sorry."

"Hello."

"CITO!"

"Tiffany, what's wrong? Why are you screaming? Is something wrong with Tree?"

Tiffany began to cry, and told Cito the call was about Diamond explaining to him what she had received at her door step.

Cito asked where she was and she answered, "Still in the house with the baby."

He put her on hold and called one of his guys to get to the house right away.

"Tiff, where is Tree?"

Between sobs, she explained to Cito what happened. Cito

understood because he knew exactly why Tree did what he did. He had lost his wife because some haters killed her to get at him. Tree knew the story and Cito understood why he was sending her away. Someone knocked on Tiffany's front door scaring her again.

"Cito someone is at the door."

Cito told her to hold on again and called his worker to make sure it was him at her door. Once he confirmed, he told Tiffany to open the door, get the baby and go with the worker. Tiffany had a question for Cito but he hung up before she could ask.

* * *

Ish's brother had been staying at Nina's house since coming to Maryland a month ago from Canada to help Ish put his plan into play. Ish walked in with a handful of gifts hoping to smooth things over since he had been gone for a while. Diamond and her baby were being held at Nina's. When he walked in Nina spit on him instantly. Ishmel was trying to be patient but he was about to punch the shit out of her.

"Nina, baby, I know you're mad and I'm sorry, but I'm trying to make a future for us."

Nina knew that was a lie because she knew he had been caked up with Autumn and showing her off around town. "Ishmel, how you think this shit is going to play out? You got Von's wife up in here and that was not part of the original plan. If he finds out, he's going to kill all our asses. Even if you let her live we're dead because she knows us both."

Ish grabbed Nina's hand and sat her down. "Look lil lady, when Shamel brought her in here she was blindfolded. We have her in a soundproof room and once it's over, we'll let her go. Everything will be over Sunday."

Nina was thinking, *you got that right motherfucker*. She had decided to see how far Ish would go with his lies. "Ish, where the fuck have you been for damn near a month?"

"Nina, you know I've been working with that bitch nigga, Oarlock, trying to make sure the Feds had enough to close their case and for me to lace you with the finer things in life without having you in hiding."

That was it for Nina, it was all she needed to hear. "Well, have you been fucking someone else because you sure haven't been fucking me Ish."

"Man, no. When do I have time Nina? Stop tripping and show me how much you've missed me."

Just as Ish got close to her someone knocked on the door. Nina thought, *good*, because she was done with Ish. He opened the door and agent Oarlock walked in. They got down to business right away. Oarlock told Ish all they had on La Familia and that was not enough to bring them down for life. The most it would get them was another two-year sentence, but they had nothing on Cito. Oarlock expressed that up till now Cito was untouchable, but if he was going to be at the buy Sunday, that would be enough. Oarlock removed a belt from his briefcase explaining to Ish that the camera and mic attached would be undetectable by those who didn't know about it. Nina sat on the couch pretending to read a book, making sure she comprehended all the info. She knew that on Sunday, Ish, Shamel, and his new crew were going to the buy together and having a roundtable discussion with Cito in attendance. This was to finalize territories with all his workers now that Von and Tree were retiring. She knew too that if she wanted to survive, as soon as they left she would have to release Diamond with a promise that she would be

OK, and Von would not seek her out later to kill her. Ish and Shamel had a drink with Oarlock to toast to their success. Nina laughed thinking, *you don't celebrate before you get the success*.

* * *

Von answered Cito's call on the first ring. "Cito we were just about to call to let you know we're on our way to meet with you."

"Von, did Tiffany call your phone? Yeah. Why, what's up?"

"Why didn't you answer her?"

"Because Tree asked me not to because she was probably looking for him, and they're going through something right now."

Cito instructed, "You two have thirty minutes to get your asses to my house."

"Cito, I know you ain't mad because I ain't want to get into their shit."

Cito hung up the phone and threw his glass against the wall. Sunshine came running into the room but backed out without a word when she saw he was OK. He didn't know how he was going to tell Von that both his wife and child were kidnapped.

Von put his phone back in his pocket and told Tree they had to get to Cito house within thirty minutes, and that Cito was pissed that they hadn't answered Tiffany's calls.

Autumn knew something was not right because Cito rarely got into any of their home business like that. Tree also suspected something else was going on and called Tiffany but got no answer. Tree and Von drove in silence. Tree loved his homeboy and wondered if he got the same vibes he and Autumn had, or if he was waiting before assuming the worse.

When they arrived at Cito's, Tree knew some shit was not right. The circular driveway was full of cars.

Von shook his head and said, "Mman your wife took this shit too far."

Tree tried to laugh it off, but he knew there was nothing funny about Cito having all these motherfuckers at his house at this late hour. He called Tiffany again, but still no answer.

"Yo Von, call Diamond and see if she answers her phone."

Von called Diamond but got no answer. "They're probably together at Cito's lying on us. You know how he is about family."

They got out of the car and Cito met them at the door looking like he had fire in his eyes. When they walked inside Ctio grabbed Von and hugged him.

Von pushed Cito off. "What's up? Yo, Cito, don't bullshit me. What the fuck are all these people doing here and you hugging me and shit? Where is my wife Cito?"

Cito told Von and Tree about the package Tiffany received and Von flipped out. He headed for the door yelling that he was going to kill anyone and everyone that had something to do with this shit. He punched walls and threw things and no one dared go near him. Tree was in shock that this shit had finally hit home. He looked at Cito for answers about his own family. Cito nodded his head toward the stairs. Tree wanted to run upstairs to hold Tiffany, but he needed to be there for his boy right now. Cito finally went to Von and held him. Von's mind was going a mile a minute wondering how he could have been so stupid to not have someone with Diamond. How could he have left her out there in the open for motherfuckers to have access to her? He pulled away from Cito and looked long and hard at Tree. Without words, Tree gathered everyone into the conference room. Von poured himself a drink but left the glass on the bar and drank straight from the bottle. He left that drink there for Diamond when she came back home.

Tree's cell phone rang. He didn't recognize the number, but figured at this time all calls needed to be answered. "Hello?"

"Tree, before you say anything or hang up, this is Nina. Now I know I am suppose to be dead and you'e probably the last person I should be calling because there's a tag on my head, but I have some info for you."

Tree gave Von and Cito a signal and put the phone on speaker because now was not a time for secrets. He signaled for everyone to be quiet, especially Von.

"Yeah Nina, what's up?"

"OK. Well, I know you know I'm alive. Well, I was saved by Ish and I've been living at a place he's keeping me in until the transfer of territory is final. Anyway, long story short, he's planning to set y'all up on Sunday. The drop is a setup. He'll be wearing a belt with a camera and a mic for the Feds. Once your meeting is over, the Feds plan to move in to get you and your father. Also, his brother is here from Canada and Tree, that nigga Shamel, is crazy as hell. Before I go I just want to tell you—I don't have a lot of time because and I'm sure Ish will be back soon—he has Diamond. His brother kidnapped her this morning coming out of the gas station."

This got the whole room's attention.

"Look Nina, I ain't playing games. Where is Diamond? A lot of niggas are getting ready to die right now."

"Tree, I want to apologize for all the shady shit I've done, but all I ask is once I give you the info, I escape with my life."

Von picked up the phone and said, "Bitch, all y'all dead. Y'all want to fuck with me and my family, my first born. Nina, I know you, you're a snake too. You tried to dead my baby in the club. If anything happens to them, you might as well kill yourself."

Nina hung up before Von could finish his threats. Tree looked at him with the urgency to shoot his ass for that outburst. Von picked up his gun and headed for the door.

Now was time for Tree to take charge. The shit was getting sloppy right before his eyes. "Von, slow your fucking roll. Man, you were wrong right there and that might have cost lives."

"Fuck you. You kept secrets from La Familia while you tried to play Magnum PI and shit. Now you want to tell me about my actions. Your family is safe."

Tree stepped to his boy like he was stepping to a nigga in the street.

"Let me tell you one thing, La Familia is always first, but while they're out there ain't no one getting sleep. Now you're acting just like I knew you would had I told you about Ish from the jump, and yet your ass don't understand why I ain't tell you. Right now you ain't right, and I am running this shit now. Like it or not, you ain't got no choice, now sit your ass down and listen."

Von punched Tree dead in the face. Tree thought about reacting like he was dealing with someone other than Von, but figured he would give Von that one. The next time he was going to take his ass out, boys or not. Tree stood up, adjusted his shirt, and rubbed his jaw. He directed four of Cito's workers to head out to VA to the house where he knew Nina had been held up. He instructed them to bring her ass to the warehouse. Tree had Evan following Ish and chirped him for his location. Evan chirped back he was at Tops Down Strip Club.

"Cool, when he walks out of that club, dead his ass. Make sure you check your surroundings for Feds because they will be watching."

Tree thought about it and changed plans. "Hold tight and just watch him. Don't let him out of your sight."

Evan chirped Tree, "Ish was not alone. He's with some cat that looks like his twin."

"Good. Look, I will hit you back in a few."

Tree chirped Autumn. "Come to Cito's house like yesterday."

She answered back, "I'm not able to because as soon as you all left, the restaurant was shot up by some of Ish's boys. I'm at the hospital with Lil Mike and it ain't looking good."

"Shit! Why you ain't call?"

"I did and no one is answering phones, not even Tiffany."

"OK, Autumn, I will be down there in a few."

FUCK! This shit done got real, real fast. "Cito, Lil Mike has been shot."

He dared Von to get up from his seat. Cito rubbed his head out of frustration because he had always held a tight ship and for someone to slip through and pretend to be loyal for so long and have this much larceny in their heart was unreal. Tree instructed Cito's head body guard to get two of his best men to watch the house all night.

Cito responded "There is no need because I have all the grounds surrounded and a guard by Tiffany's door."

He loaded his guns and handed Ice his car keys. His head bodyguard stopped Ice and instructed him to take one of the security cars with hidden compartments, loaded guns, and bullet proof vests. Ice handed him Tree's car keys, took the security keys and headed out to bring the car around. Von was in a stupor but still drinking Crown Royal from the bottle, his eyes as red as blood and at a lost as to what to do.

Tree finally ran upstairs to see his wife and daughter before he headed out. When he walked into the room Tiffany ran into his arms and cried. She quickly asked if her cousin was dead. Tree held her because he couldn't answer her question. He lifted her head to look into her eyes. It was not until she looked at him fully that she noticed he had on a bulletproof vest and both of his guns. She stepped back and sat on the bed to gather her thoughts. Her world was falling apart slowly and there was nothing she could do about it. Tree went over to the crib and looked at his daughter who was sleeping peacefully. He picked her up, held her close to him, kissed her, and put her back in the crib. On his way out, he took her bear that was in the crib and placed it in his vest next to his heart. He held Tiffany's hand as he walked toward the door, told her he loved her, but he did not have the heart to tell her about her brother, he would let Cito tell her. Tiffany held on a little while longer, let his hand go, and watched her husband walk out hoping it was not the last time she would see him.

Chapter TWENTY-EIGHT

Diamond was hurting bad. Shamel had put a beating on her and she vowed to herself that if she made it out of that room and got him alone she was going to kill him.

She had stopped to get gas off hwy 64 when a van pulled up, a guy from the back seat snatched her up, another guy grabbed her baby, and a third one pulled off in her car. It happened so fast she had no time to reach under her seat for her .42. She should have just gone to her cousin's house, like she had planned, to let her know what was going on and see if she wanted to ride out too. But then again, both of them would be in this situation instead of just her.

Diamond picked up her daughter who had been crying for awhile because she didn't have a bottle for her, she hoped like hell her breast had not fully dried up. When the baby stopped crying, Diamond listened intensely for sounds from outside, but heard none. She knew her forehead was bleeding but she was afraid to let her guard down and ask for help. Besides, she feared being attacked again and was not prepared to fight. Just as she put the baby down the door opened.

Diamond couldn't see the face of the person in the door because it was too dark and the person wore a hood. A tray was slid into the room and the door immediately slammed shut. Reluctant to go near the door, she waited awhile before examining the tray. To her surprise, there were a couple of cans of formula, new bottles, food and snacks on the tray. She was getting pissed now because she really wanted to know who this person was that was holding her and her new baby captive in a room with no lights and not showing their face. Suddenly a light came on in the room and Diamond prepared herself to fight her way out if need be. Waiting, the door never opened, but with a little light she noticed a letter on the tray. This had to be some kind of fucking joke and if it was, Diamond was not laughing. She was ready to kill whoever was behind this. It had been several hours and she knew that the set up was scheduled for tomorrow. Diamond finally decided to read the letter while the lights were still on. Straining under dim lights, she read:

> *Diamond,*
>
> *I know I am the last person you want to hear from being that our history is one of bad blood. I have done a lot of foul stuff in the past and for that I will pay in the next life. Enough of that, let's get down to business. Diamond, the person behind all this drama and the person setting up your husband and La Familia is the same one that played me and now I'm ready to get even. I know if let you out without explaining myself, you will surely try your best to kill me. So let me lay down how I want this plan to work to ensure that Ish gets what's coming to him and I can make it out safe. I called Tree to work with him, but I fear for my life after your husband's threat to kill me. Ish has been working with FBI Agent Oarlock, who*

is grimy too. He once tried to get down with Cito back in the day, but Cito was not hearing him and wanted to do his thing solo. Since then, there's been this bad blood. Why Ish is crossing La Familia, I don't know, but why I'm crossing him is clear. Although he saved my life the night Tree wanted me killed alongside Jay, he played me and has been hanging out with some chick named Autumn. Although I'm sure she doesn't know anything about me, an ass whoppin is sure to come to her just on GP. You probably can't feel me on it, but that is for another time. The drop is Sunday, and if I let you out of here I have a plan to make sure that Ish nor Oarlock make it to the drop and La Familia is safe. I have been sleeping with Oarlock and Ish's brother behind Ish's back for a month now, so it is no big thing to get rid of them. The first and most dangerous of the two is Shamel. So look Diamond, Shamel is due here tonight around midnight. You'll find a watch under the cereal box. Right before he gets here I will unlock your door. I'll take him to bed and keep him occupied. I left a gun in the kitchen in the second drawer, near the window. A silencer is already on it. You know what to do from there. I'm going to take you at your word if you acknowledge the letter by sliding it back under the door…meaning we're working together. If the letter is passed, I will slide you a cell—but it only has five minutes on it—to let Von know you're OK. Please, I am trusting you that you will not have them kill me and let me get away in one piece. As for Oarlock, once Shamel is dead and if I survive, I will tell you the rest of the information Von and Tree will need on him.

Diamond folded the letter after reading it twice to make

sure she was reading it right. She leaned against the wall and thought about what Nina said in the letter. It didn't take a rocket scientist to know who wrote it, now the thing was could she really be trusted. Hell, she was the same one that killed her own sister over a man and what about Autumn? She wants to do harm to her and that's not happening. Diamond folded the letter, slid it under the door and waited to see if she would follow through with the cell. Nina smiled when she saw the letter and knew no blood would be on her hands on this one, but she was sure to cause a lot of blood shed to many others based on the chain of events she was about to set in motion. Nina slid the phone under the door. Diamond hurried up and made the call to Von, trying to make sure she had everything she needed to say lined up so she could get it out in five minutes.

Von had been drinking a lot in the last twenty four hours and getting furious that Tree was having meetings and planning how to straighten this whole situation and not asking his opinion. Von felt Tree was in it for self and was not thinking about the fact that this was his wife they had, not his. Von had never had ill feelings towards Tree in all the years they had been on the grind. Sure they had had some heated arguments and even shot the fair one in the streets, but after they got things off their chest they were back good. This time though, Von felt he was being played and treated like a worker instead of one of the heads of all La Familia had built. He was about to call in a few favors of his own to some people he was cool with and do his own thing to get his family back and take care of Ish and anyone who had been involved with him. Tree had allowed Ish to live too long. Yeah, he was down with the plan to sit back and let Autumn do her job but the game had flipped. Hands had been laid on his family and for that, there was no coming back. Just then, Von's phone rang. He didn't know the number, but at this point it ain't really matter.

"Who the Fuck is this?" Von answered through slurred speech.

"Baby it's me and I only have 5 minutes, so listen careful. Don't make any moves, I am good and I will get back at you. No one has touched me. Keep with what you got going on your end, and I got me. I love you and no matter what, I ride with you for life."

Von sat in awe with his mouth wide open and before he could speak, the line went dead. He became sober instantly after the call, ran immediately up stairs to Tiffany's room and entered without even knocking. Tiffany was startled at first, but calmed down when she realized it was Von. She could see he was going through the same hell she was in. How was this happening? How did they allow someone to get so close to her cousin, and how could they not know that Ish was a snake? She knew she should have never gotten involved with someone in the game again. She had been strong about not doing that and now look at her held up in a house with her newborn, fearing the worst.

Von questioned Tiffany, "Have you heard from Diamond?"

"No, Von, I haven't."

She searched his face a little longer and asked, "Do you know where she is?"

Von searched her face as well, and could see the pain and anger. Von sighed, sat on the edge of the bed with his hands folded and said, "I just got a weird call from her stating for me to do what was planned and that she's got her end."

Tiffany decided to ask the question that she had been wondering about for the past eight hours. "Von, what is the plan?"

Von laid it out for her the best he knew. He told her that Tree knew Nina has something to do with some of it because he got a call from her stating that she wanted to help get back at Ish because he was dirty and did her dirty, but he has not moved on her yet. Tiffany was confused because she remembered when they found out Ish was a traitor. Tree followed him and learned that Nina was alive and where she lived in VA. Again, she wondered if he still had feelings for her and this was the reason he didn't have her killed. Tiff decided to keep listening instead of speaking her thoughts out loud. Von went on to tell her that Cito and Tree have planned the drop to take place on Sunday, but not the drop Oarlock expects. Being that some of the officers are on Cito's roll, they want to set it up for a shoot out to take place with Oarlock not making it out. Ish will never make it to the drop because Autumn is to handle him Sunday right before the drop. This gives them time to go in, get the body, and dispose of it at the meeting spot to make it look like he was shot by Oarlock during the shoot out. His concern was that he and Tree will have to leave the states for a month or two until things calm down because they are not sure who all the players are in this and if they will still be charged with something if they hang around with a dead cop popping up who was working on a case with their names involved.

Tiffany was pissed because first, she had to hear about Lil Mike from Cito, and now, Tree failed to mention anything to her about leaving the states. Hell, her brother, Lil Mike, was still in the hospital and she could not be there for him. She was dammed if she was leaving the states.

Von sensed Tiffany was in thought and asked, "What's on your mind.

She told him all she was thinking.

Von laughed a little and said, "Tiff, as mad as I am at that man right now for dragging his feet, I can truly say that Nina means nothing to him. You know your husband, unlike the rest of us, is a deep man and he thinks a lot of his stuff out before he acts on it. Hell, he's got Cito in check because he has literally taken over. He knows me and Cito are hot heads and we have our guns ready to make this thing go down like the wild west. As drunk as I have been, many thoughts of hate have gone through my mind about that man and I know that they ain't justified. It's just my ignorance and hot temper and I know I will respect it in the end when I'm able to see results. As for going out of the states, well sorry Ma, but y'all will not be going on this trip."

Tiffany looked Von square in the eyes and asked, "What you mean we will not be going? Y'all ain't single no more and this ain't no solo show, y'all got wives and children now."

Von responded, "And because of that y'all ain't going. Y'all are safer here holding us down than you are with us."

Tiffany started to say something but gave him a sinister grin instead, and said, "OK Von, I will let Diamond handle this one. She's been chilling these last couple hours while we've been stressed, so she needs to have some work when she gets home."

Von smiled. "I'll remember to tell her that."

Just then, Tree walked in and looked from Von to Tiffany trying to figure out why he was in the room with her and what they were talking about.

"Yo, what's up? What y'all in here kicking it about?"

"Nothing man, just needed to talk to someone and since everyone seemed busy and was leaving me out the loop, I figured why not go to the only other person out the loop." Von stood and left the room so Tree and Tiffany could talk in private.

Tree knew what Von was going through, but his smart ass mouth was getting on Tree's last nerve. He was testing him and Tree was even feeling a little disrespected. Had it been any other person in the street to come at him like Von had, they would be dead and stinking right where they stood. Tree turned his attention back to his wife who had walked away and had her back turned to him. He asked her what that was all about and she responded by slapping him so hard it hurt her hand and of course, stung his face. Tree had had enough of the bull shit with Tiffany and Von. He hauled off and slapped her ass back.

"That was the second and last time with that slap shit. What the fuck is wrong with you?"

Tree wanted to fight someone. He was so stressed out and his own wife was giving him shit. Hell no, it was about to stop right now. Before she could answer, Tree tossed her ass on the bed, jumped on her and squeezed her face so hard he felt his fingers leaving prints in her cheeks.

Tiffany was now crying uncontrollably because she couldn't believe she had laid hands on her husband and he had slapped her back. What was going on that they were hitting on each other?

Tree let go and rolled off of her shaking his head in disbelief. Sure he had placed his hands on a couple of females with no regrets, but he never once thought about laying hands on his wife.

"Tiffany, what's the problem Ma, why you tripping on me? How you just going to slap a nigga? Tiff, I never laid hands on you, and I ask you a question and you slap me?

What part of the game is that? Answer me!!!"

His yelling made Tiffany jumpy and woke the baby. Tiffany spoke softly. "Tree, why didn't you tell me you were going to have to leave the states and leave me and your daughter behind? Why am I left in the dark? You got a call from Nina and you know where she lives, yet she's still living and probably has something to do with my cousin's disappearance and yet my cousin ain't home, Tree. So tell me why am I in the dark? In case you forgot I'm your fucking wife."

Now Tiffany's whispers were becoming yells. Tree laughed at the fact that Von had reduced himself to a bitch by coming in and telling the plan to his wife. Tiffany was confused as to why Tree found anything she was saying funny. Tree had had enough. He stood up, straightened his clothes, kissed his daughter and headed towards the door. Tiffany was not having it. If you walk out that door I will not be here when you get back. Tree turned, smiled at her, and said something he never thought he would say to her, but he had to gain back control.

"Tiffany, if that's how you feel, then get the fuck on, but make sure you know not to try to walk out of here with my daughter. You're free to do what you got to for you, but my daughter stays." Tiffany was stunned as Tree continued ranting. "And while I'm thinking about it, maybe that's best…if what I do for you ain't good enough then Tiffany, get the fuck, gone. Last, but not least, I'll straighten Von's ass for coming in here like a punk and reducing himself the way he did by coming to you. But if you leave, as much as I love you and would die for you, just keep it moving because you can never come back."

He walked over to Tiffany and she flinched when he got near her because she thought he was going to hit her. But he simply took her face into his hands, kissed her on her forehead, told her he loved her, and walked out. Tiffany stood immobile for several minutes. How did her good life turn into what was now going on?

Chapter TWENTY-NINE

Tree couldn't believe Von tried to play his wife against him. He took the stairs two at a time making all the security turn their heads trying to figure out what the urgency was. With their hands near their guns in the event they needed to draw, they followed closely behind Tree to the den. Cito and Von were talking when Tree walked up to Von and told him to get his bitch ass up. Von ignored and continued talking. Before he could get his next words out, Tree hit him in the head with the butt of his gun. He stepped back, giving Von enough room to stand up once he got his composure, but Cito immediately jumped between them. Tree's eyes were red as if he'd just smoked a blunt. Cito asked what was going on, but in Tree's mind, now was not the time for the father bull shit…this was between them and he was going to beat Von's ass like he was that disrespectful nigga Ish.

Von charged at Tree but he moved before his body made contact. Tree, in return, punched Von square in his mouth and every chance he got. he hit him again in the mouth. Tree was making a point to remind Von about snitch niggas and bitch niggas that just love to run their mouths. Von knew the code in the street, and after a few rounds Tree walked away not having the energy to fight him anymore. Reason being, Von was not fighting back because he got the message Tree was delivering. But with a bloody mouth, Von decided to express his anger.

"So does that make you feel like a big man now, Tree? Oh, you're the boss, now fuck me and Cito. Everything is what you say, huh? And when someone in the La Familia crosses you this is how you handle it? Your ass is selfish and everything is about you. You don't give a shit about the rest of us. Now I see why Ish turned on your ass. You lead us to believe that you're about La Familia, but you ain't shit, Tree. Your perfect little family, oh they're safe and sound, so just take your sweet fucking time finding mine and handling the shit. And you don't even have enough respect for me to give me the man power to handle the shit on my own. You instruct your crew to fall back until you say go. Yeah, all about you. Look at you. You don't even respect me enough right now to face me…you give me your back to talk to. You're a coward nigga. You talk a good game about the streets but you don't honor the code."

Cito walked over to Von. "Don't do this."

Von shrugged Cito's hand off. "See Tree, you even got the old man defending you, like you're really the king. Well guess what, you ain't shit. And I don't need the so-called La Familia because ain't nothing La Familia can do about this shit, it's all you. You went to Georgia to set up shop there and without asking me, you just told me what you were going to do and what my role was, and I went with it. Cito did too. Then you come back here after I had been working these streets on my own for a year, and you want to just take over, and fuck me? Naw nigga...fuck you. I am done! You hear that Tree, I am done! Out of respect for Cito is the only reason that you're still living. You know who the real leader is in this thing. I fell back because Cito asked me, but now nigga, I'm in charge. Do you hear me?! You better not breathe unless I say so. And as for Sunday, the plans have changed. All them niggas that decided to disrespect the so called La Familia will be dead before the sun comes up on Sunday."

Tree was torn up inside that his so-called brother and best friend had felt all this larceny in his heart for him and all the while smiling in his face and breaking bread with him. His blood was boiling that Von was trying him and threatening to kill him. He finally turned around, stared Von in the eyes and got so close to him they could feel each others breath. Von knew he had crossed the line again big time, but there was no turning back. Tree spoke between clinched teeth. "You know Von, I am sorry you felt that way and had to be the same undercover snake and bitch that Ish turned out to be with all that hate and resentment in your heart for me. But if it is a war you want with me, then do what you got to, but we both know idle threats are for people with no real heart. So it is clear to me that you have no heart or you really intend to try to kill me. Either way, if you feel that going to war in these streets with Ish and the FBI is the right thing to do and will get your family back safe and fast, then do you. I wish you luck on it. On the strength of Diamond and your seed, I got La Familia's back on this one. But as for me and you nigga, you're dead in my eyes. And once I walk out this door, if you ever see me in the street and you try me like you have today, your wife will be burying your ass six feet under."

Tree backed up, went to Cito, shook his hand, thanked him for everything he has ever done for him, and vowed to end his relationship with the La Familia. He walked out of Cito's house for what would probably be the last time. Tiffany had been sitting at the top of the stairs listening to the whole thing go down and was in tears yet again.

Cito was in disbelief at what had just gone down. Where had everything gone so wrong? This shit was out of control and it was time for Cito to stop acting like an old man and claim is rightful place in this business. All that was happening now would have never taken place in his day because a snake or snitch would be dead before they even knew that they were one. Cito signaled his lieutenant who knew what was up without words being spoken. Cito went into his office, had a couple of shots of Patron and called Sunshine to come in and relieve some of his stress before he ended all this nonsense in the street. He needed to regain the relationship between the two boys he had raised as his sons and who he thought loved each other as brothers.

Tiffany entered Cito's office and asked to speak to him. He motioned for her to sit in the chair in front of him and excused Sunshine from the room. Tiffany was visibly upset, but now was not the time for Cito to play the comforting father. He had other shit to take care of, and fast.

"Cito, look, I saw everything that went down and I'm always going to side with my husband. What I just want to ask you is to make sure that at the end of all of this, both of them come home safe."

Cito poured both of them a shot. "I will make sure everything is back the way it's suppose to be."

Tiffany was somewhat satisfied, but asked one more question. "Cito, do you think Sunshine would watch the baby for a few while I look for Tree?"

"I don't think that is the best idea for you to leave the

house. Diamond's life is already at stake, I don't need the headache of two of y'all out there"

"I understand, but I have my .45, I'll keep in touch and shoot anyone that gets near me. If you like, I'll even go with one of your workers, and once I find him they can come back and I'll stay with Tree."

Cito turned his back to her and without his verbal consent, she went to find Sunshine.

Tree could not believe the shit that had gone down at the house. Aanother mother fucker turned out to be a stab in the back—his brother. They came into this shit together and when some real shit comes down on them, instead of sticking together they crumpled like some dry ass bread. Tree's phone rang and brought him to the realization that he had left the house heated and left his wife and child. He was cussing himself for not having them on his mind and not taking them with him. He knew that Von would never hurt them but, then again, he never figured Von would turn on him like he did. He turned the car around as he answered the phone.

"Yo, Tiff, I'm on my way to get you right now, have the baby ready."

"Tree, I'm not taking the baby with me but, we need to talk. Call me when you're outside, I'll be waiting for you."

Tree held the phone away from his ear as if he was hearing a foreign language, took a breath, and said, "Look Tiff, I don't want y'all in that house another second."

Tiffany and Tree had been arguing a lot since Diamond had been missing, but now was not the time and what he was saying right now was not even an option.

She said, "I'll be waiting," and hung up the phone.

Tiffany left the house with only her gun in the small of her back. She jumped in the car and leaned over to kiss Tree, but he pulled back and asked her where the fuck his daughter was.

Tiffany said, "I already told you…we need to talk. You know nothing is going to happen to her in that house so you need to chill."

Tree drove off but was clueless as where they were going.

"Look Tree, I want to first start off by saying I know you're under a lot of stress, but if you ever put your hands on me again, you better make sure you dial 911 right before you do because I will try my best to kill you."

Tree had known he was wrong so he didn't bother to respond to her, even though both times she had struck him first.

"Second Tree, I am with you all the way on anything you do because you are my husband and my soul mate, but don't keep secrets from me ever. The one feeling that is the worse in the world is having someone tell you something about your man or women and you're clueless."

Tree pulled into the same hotel that he and Tiffany had sealed their relationship at. He opened her door and handed the valet his key. After checking in and getting into their room, Tree didn't bother to speak his sorrow to his wife. He decided to let their bodies do the talking. He wanted to show her that he was truly sorry and that is what he did. He made love to his wife like it would be the last time they would ever be together. Tiffany cried that night because she could feel her husband's pain, and she was worried about him and the outcome of tomorrow's meeting. What if they really went to war in the streets? She could not see herself living without this man and only being able to tell their daughter stories of her father and the man he was. She held on to him like she already knew what he was feeling and thinking. Eventually they drifted off to sleep with their bodies intertwined.

Around 4 AM, Tree's phone rang. He looked at the screen and thought his mind was playing tricks on him because Nina couldn't be dumb enough to call when she knew her life was in danger for her dealings with Ish, and the fact that she knew he had something to do with Diamond and the baby being kidnapped.

"Hello."

Diamond could hear the sleep in Tree's voice.

"Tree, it's me, Diamond. I tried calling Von but his phone went into voicemail."

Tree jumped up hurriedly, and reached for Tiffany, hoping he had not knocked her to the floor. "Diamond, are you OK?"

"Yeah, I'm fine. All I know is that I'm at Nina's house, but I'm not exactly sure where that is. Nina had me agree to work with her to take Ish and his brother out. She and his brother are in the bedroom now and I'm supposed to go in and shoot him. I know you know where she lives so get here as soon as possible." With that, she hung up.

Tree wasn't sure if this was a set up but he knew he had to go. He jumped up, put his clothes on and made a quick call to Autumn at the same time.

"Yo, that nigga Ish with you?"

"No. He said he was going to his crib to get some clothes and would be back."

"Check it, I need you to make sure his ass doesn't leave your sight for a while. I'll explain it to you later. There's a lot of shit that's about to go down, so please make sure you're near your phone at all times. I will hit you in an hour." Before Tree hung up he reminded Autumn he loved her like a sister.

Autumn was puzzled and felt the need to call Von. Never

had either of them spoken I love you's because it was always known. Tree called Lil Mike's road dog, Kesahn because at this point, he was not trusting anyone that was working for him and Von. Deep in his heart he knew he should have called Cito and got message to Von, but fuck it.

"Yo, Kesahn, meet me at the spot in five minutes. Don't be late nigga."

Kesahn ain't even ask what was going on. He just rolled out of bed, put his clothes on, grabbed his .9 and a blunt and rolled out.

Once they met up at the spot, Tree informed him about what was going on. Kesahn, a man of few words, handed Tree the blunt to hit, turned up the music, and waited for Tree to roll out. When they got to Nina's they proceeded to the door very slowly.

Tree called Autumn back to see if Ish was back at her crib. Autumn let him know that he was, in a round about way, and ended the call.

Tree turned the knob slowly and walked into Nina's place cautiously. It had an eerie silence to it. Kesahn walked to the back of the house and saw a dead man on the bed and a woman tied to the bedpost. He backed up and felt a gun to his head. Not wanting to be to fast, he held his hands up slow and let go of his gun.

At the same time, Tree came down the hall, saw Diamond and called out her name. When she saw Tree, she let her gun down slow and began sobbing. He put his Polo jacket across her shoulders and held her.

Kesahn picked up his gun and asked Diamond, "Where's the baby?"

She pointed to the door at the end of the hall. He put his gun in his pants and picked up the baby. Tree looked in the room and saw Nina tied up and looking high as hell. He was not sure how to play this because Diamond had the chance to kill her but she was still alive. Tree pulled away from Diamond and ordered her to take the baby the car with Kesahn.

"I'll take care of this business in here."

He walked into the room, took the tape off Nina's mouth and untied her. Nina was shaking because she wasn't sure what was going to happen next and because she was so high she really didn't give a fuck at this point.

"Nina, why did you come back here if you were safe?"

Nina ignored his question, looked at the dead body in her bed, then looked at the clock.

"Look Tree, Oarlock and his people are due to meet here in about an hour to go over the final plans for tomorrow's meeting."

"OK, get yourself together so you are ready for them. Is this nigga supposed to be at this meeting tonight with them?"

"No."

Tree rolled Shamel up in the blanket, pulled the area rug up on the bed and rolled the body in it. Nina, open the door to the room they had Diamond stashed in. Nina did as she was told, and Tree stuck the body in there and propped it up like he was Diamond sitting there. To make sure they got the affect that it was Diamond he asked Nina to give him one of her many wigs that was close to what Diamond's hair looks like. He rolled towels in the baby's blanket, placed it in Shamel's hands and shut the door.

"Nina, act like nothing happened and I will call you in about an hour or two, to get the final game plan." He turned to Nina on his way out and said, "If you try to run before you help me, I will find you. On the strength of you helping

Diamond and her baby, you get to live another day. Don't fuck with me Nina, because this time I will make sure that you are good and dead, unlike how I depended on someone else to make sure you were before."

Nina didn't respond and at that point knew she deserved to die because she had done some ill shit. At that moment, she was grateful that both Tree and Diamond had spared her life just a little while longer because she had one more person to get even with before she died.

Tree got in the car and drove Diamond to Cito's house. When they arrived he did not get out the car and Diamond was a little confused about it but was so happy to be back on La Familia territory that she didn't bother to ask why. When he saw someone open the door, he and Kesahn pulled off.

Chapter THIRTY

When Von opened the door he cried as if he was a baby. He was so happy to be looking in the face of his wife and baby that he could not move. He saw Tree's car leaving the driveway. Cito was walking down the hall and stopped in his tracks when he saw who was standing at the door. Von pulled Diamond into him and held her. Cito pulled them in the house and out of the door before someone noticed them that shouldn't.

Von looked them over, asked if they were OK, and how she ended up with Tree. She explained what happened. "I called your phone and it went to voicemail. I was able to reach Tree and he rescued me at Nina's. I had to kill Shamel."

Von felt like shit. After everything he had said and done that night, Tree still represented and saved his family.

"Diamond, take the baby upstairs to her room and the two of you get comfortable."

Cito then turned to Von, "Get your ass in the office right now!"

Von responded, "Whatever you have to say can wait because I want to be with my wife right now."

Cito got in his face and said, "I ain't asking you shit, I'm telling you to get your ass in the office right now."

Von had seen some bad sides of Cito, but the look in his eyes right now spoke volumes. In the office, Cito hauled off and punched Von square in the face. Von bent over in pain.

"Now that that's out of the way, let's get down to business. You crossed the line earlier. I am in control of this shit and at the end of the day, y'all motherfuckers work for me…you owe me. I don't want to think that you are a snake and that you have real larceny in your heart for a man you call your brother, but today your actions showed that. I really want to believe that all your threats and words were those of hurt because of your situation, but even then we are to stick together, not turn on each other. That man came to you as just that, a man, and told you up front why he did not come to us until he was sure and I respected that. Why couldn't you? You know why you couldn't? Because you thought you were the boss. You know Tree would allow nothing to happen to your people or you. Tonight after all was said and done, you should have been at the phone keeping camp. But instead, that same man you wanted to kill rescued your wife when she called and did not second guess it. He left his own and put himself on the line for you and yours with no help from any of us. You know why? Well probably because of your bullshit today, he didn't feel comfortable enough to call and ask for help to rescue your family, because he didn't know who to trust. I'm sure he felt he was probably being set up.

You fix this shit and you fix it fast. I don't know how you're going to do it and I don't give a shit, but you do it. This shit is not about favorites…before you open your mouth to say it and get hit again. Now you're dismissed."

"Cito!"

"I said get the fuck out, you're dismissed. Go spend time with your wife, get your mind right for tomorrow and fix the bullshit."

Cito turned in his seat and looked out the window. He was not one to cry, but his heart was heavy. His lieutenant entered the room to inform him everything was set up for tomorrow, and everyone knew their position. Cito asked him to arrange a last minute meeting with the crew before morning. Tomorrow would be the first time in years that he had actually been out doing dirty work, but he had to go back to the streets...back to his roots. He was who the Fed's really wanted. Shit, his name had been out there for a long time and if serving time or taking a bullet was going to save the only real family he had, well, he guessed that was what he had to do. Tomorrow would make or break what was known as La Familia.

G STREET CHRONICLES
~A NEW URBAN DYNASTY~

WWW.GSTREETCHRONICLES.COM

Chapter THIRTY-ONE

A utumn was sick of the shit and she felt that Tree and Von were dragging their feet and she was tired of entertaining this lame nigga when her real man was still laid up in the hospital. Lil Mike had finally made it out of ICU and was improving. Autumn felt she needed to be with him more than smiling in Ish's face.

Ish was sitting in the corner in his boxers counting money. "Yo, Autumn, tomorrow I will be the real king in these streets, and you know who you'll be? The mother fucking queen at my side. People are about to hate on us big time."

Autumn asked, "Is everything covered for tomorrow with security and shit?"

"Well, Ma, I've recruited a new crew out of New York that worked with my brother. Right now they're camped in VA, and should be arriving soon. Matter fact, I wonder what the fuck is up with Shamel, I ain't heard from his ass all day."

Autumn already knew why he hadn't heard from him. Tree called earlier and updated her on everything about the fight with Von, Diamond killing Shamel and Diamond being back at home.

"Well what about the Fed dude? Can you trust him?"

"Yeah, he's got a lot at stake here because he's going to take Cito down, make himself look good, and we'll split the business. He's going to work as my silent partner, so to speak."

Autumn was thinking, *this nigga really doesn't see anything wrong with what the fuck he's getting ready to do.* "Well do you need me to do anything to help you out tomorrow, because you know I stay strapped?"

Ish smiled and said, "Naw, but I will need you to help me get rid of Von's wife's body once the meeting is over. I will have no use for her after Von and Tree's asses are either locked up or dead tomorrow, depending on how they decide they want to go out. Diamond always had mouth and a trigger happy finger, so she'll come after me if I let her live."

Autumn was OK with his plans because little did Ish know, Diamond was not the one going to die tomorrow and hopefully, neither was Tree or Von.

* * *

Diamond was so happy to be in Von's arms again that she couldn't let go of him. She noticed his bruised lips and face and asked, "What the fuck happened to you?"

"Man, shit went wrong D when you were kidnapped." Von told Diamond all about his fight with Tree and how Cito had punched him in the face. Diamond was in a state of shock and could not believe Von had flipped out on family. She had never seen that side of Von other than when they had their own troubles but to turn on his boy with jealousy was something new for her.

"Well, what the fuck were you thinking? You know how you are, you have known this nigga all your life and you know he would never do anything that would hurt you or me." Diamond was pissed. "So now what, Von? You have a meeting tomorrow with that snake ass, Ish, and that crooked ass cop and now the family is at odds? So you going in alone?"

Von shook his head really not needing the argument at the time. He had a lot of shit on his mind and was overwhelmed with having his family back.

"Look D, I don't know what's going to happen right now with tomorrow and you are right, I fucked up. But I can't dwell on the past and how to fix the shit right now. All I can do is go by what Cito has planned and hope we all make it out. I'll mend the shit with me and Tree later."

Diamond was not content with that plan and dialed Tree's number. Tiffany answered his phone after it rang several times. "Hello?"

"Hey Tiff, it's me Diamond."

Tiffany was at a loss of words hearing her cousin's voice. "Are you OK? Where are you?"

"I'm at Cito's house with Von, didn't Tree tell you? He was the one who rescued me from Nina's house because Von wasn't answering his phone when I called for help."

It was 4 PM, and Tiffany had wondered why he was still sleep at this time of the day, but that would explain it. "No, when I woke up he was here sleeping. I didn't even know he had gone out. Well, I'm on my way there to assure myself that you're OK."

Diamond stopped her and asked, "Tiff, what happened with Von and Tree?"

Tiffany explained what she had witnessed and what Von told her when he came to her room drunk. Diamond was stunned because again she could not believe this was her husband.

"Tiff, is Tree there with you? Yeah, but he's sleep."

"Well, can you wake him up? It's important that I speak to him and they need to resolve this mess before the meeting tonight."

Tiffany didn't want to wake Tree. "I'm going to let him sleep a little longer and then bring him over. They are having a meeting anyway at 7:00 and Kennedy is still there."

Diamond had been so wrapped up in being home and all that had taken place, she had not even thought to ask about the baby.

"She's here?"

"Yeah, Sunshine is watching her for me. I just needed some time alone with Tree because we had a little falling out of our own."

Diamond sighed and asked, "Well who the fuck is Sunshine?"

Tiffany laughed. "You are so slow and out of the times. She is one of Cito's main jump-off's."

They both laughed.

Diamond said, "Well I see he still got it going on. Hell, I stopped keeping up because at one time he had the doors revolving like a hotel with different women. Well, I'm going to take a long overdue bath and get my child straight, then check on Kennedy because I don't know this Sunshine chick, and I want to make sure she ain't trying to hurt my little cousin. I'll see you in a couple of hours.

"Diamond, I'm so happy you're safe and I can't wait to see you and my little cousin."

When Diamond returned to Von, he was immediately defensive and gave her a hand sign to listen to him. Look D, before you come in trying to judge what I did, you have to understand that Tree has always been my equal, so for him to flip the game and take charge was something new for me. I thought he was trying to take over and cut me out or some shit, and Cito was on his side.

Diamond gave him the hand sign, and said, Look, I don't know what type of bad shit you been smoking and I don't give a damn. You're acting real weak right now and I don't know who you are. All I have to say is get your mind right and man up. What have you done with the plan you started with Autumn in the mix?"

"Von said she's still boo'ing him up."

Diamond said, "Like I assumed…nothing? Had you let her kill his ass when she asked, I wouldn't have been kidnapped and your daughter endangered."

Von stood up and shouted at her, "Look, don't put all this shit on me. Had your boy killed his ass as soon as he found out he was a fucking snitch, none of us would be stressing right now. Not to mention this is the man he picked to put in the spot to take over the territory that we built. So you and everyone else can kiss my ass."

Von grabbed his jacket, walked pass Diamond and left. She wanted to go after him but figured fuck it…I will take care of some of this shit myself. She went in to check on Kennedy who was being rocked and fed by an unfamiliar woman.

"You must be Sunshine?"

Sunshine acknowledged her with a beautiful smile. She obviously was not as young as Diamond and Tiffany, but surely not as old as Cito. "Yes I am, and judging by your looks, you must be Tiffany's cousin, Diamond. You guys could pass for sisters, you look so much alike."

Diamond smiled and asked to hold the baby.

"Does your cousin know you're here?"

"Yes, I talked to her a few minutes ago. She'll be here soon to get the baby."

Sunshine could tell Diamond was tired as she hugged Kennedy lovingly and close to her before giving her back. "It was nice to meet you Sunshine. How long will you be in town?"

"I'm not sure. I have a couple of things to take care of before I leave, but I'm sure I will see you before I leave."

Diamond took a long bath with water as hot as she could stand it. Afterwards, she got dressed in a Donna Karan sweat suit with matching Donna Karan sneakers. She woke the baby, bathed and fed her, then called her mother.

"Hey Ma, how are you?"

"I am good baby, how about you?"

"I'm fine. I know this is last minute, but I was just wondering if you could come get the baby?"

"Diamond, are you asking me to fly there for the baby and return immediately? What is really going on? Look Ma, it's something that does not need to be discussed over the phone, but I really need this favor from you more then anything. As a matter of fact, if you can take both babies, I promise you I will explain everything later. Mom, it really is important that they're picked up immediately. Von is ending his relationship in the business, and it is best the children are not here."

Her mother always hated the line of work Von was in, but she tried to mind her business. "Well, what time would I catch a flight?"

"Actually mommy, what I'm going to do is have Cito send his jet to get you, meet you at the airport, and you'll do an immediate return. So if you could be at Rock Hill Airport in about two hours, that will work."

Her mother gave a deep sigh, and agreed. "I'm bringing your aunt with me because you know good and well I can't handle two infants. And another thing Diamond, when all this shit is over you need to concentrate on being a mother. Y'all street days are over. You all had a good run, made a lot of money and, to date, no one has gone to jail. But I feel it in my heart that something ain't right and something is going to happen if you don't get out now."

Diamond knew her mother was right and she always had visions of things happening long before they happened.

"Mommy, you're right, and if you would pray for all of us tonight that we make it out in one piece, I promise you this is it. Even if Von doesn't stop, I am willing to walk away from this marriage and be a mother for my daughter. Anyway Mommy, please go and get ready for the flight, I need to get the kids ready."

Diamond hung up from her mother, went downstairs to talk to Cito, and ran into Monty, Cito's lieutenant.

"Hey Monty, how are you?"

He was so happy to see her safe. "Girl get over here and give me a hug."

Monty and Cito were cousins and he had been down with Cito from the beginning, all the way to the top, and thought of all of them as his children just like Cito. Diamond hugged Monty and asked, "Is the old man available, I need to ask a favor?"

"Well before you ask him, how about you run it pass me first…you know he's got a lot on his plate right now."

"OK, well I was wondering if the jet could be chartered to Rock Hill to pick up my mommy and aunt to take the babies back with them."

Monty asked, "Don't you think you and Tiff need to be

on that flight too?"

Diamond smiled, "You know I'm a rider, and I am not about to leave my husband among snakes in the battle he is about to go into. I have already started shining my .9 and .45, got my vest out and even picked out a hot outfit."

Monty laughed, "You are a trip." He got on his walkie-talkie and arranged for the jets roundtrip.

When the arrangements were finalized he said, "Miss Lady, your wish has been granted. Is there anything else that I can do for you?"

Diamond kissed him on his cheek and said, "For now, I think that will do. I need to get the little ones ready and call Tiffany to come see her baby before she leaves because I made all the decisions on this one without talking to her about it."

Monty laughed and said, "Well good luck on dealing with Tiffany, after you tell her you're sending her bambino away."

"You know I'm in charge. Tiffany will get knocked out if she wants to act the fool."

"Knocked out for what? I just walked in the door and you're talking shit!"

Diamond turned to her cousin and back at Monty and said, "You set me up."

Monty threw his hands up surrendering and walked away. Diamond hugged Tiffany and pulled her up the stairs. Man, I missed you. Tiffany said, Girl, you need to have been on your game. How did you just let someone come up and snatch you? I thought I taught you better then that. They both laughed. Diamond told her the plan to send the babies to Charlotte until the smoke cleared.

Tiffany said, "Well thanks for asking me."

"Yeah, well you were trying to be happy and sad about me and then being boo'd up with your husband. I couldn't wait for you to come up for air, I had to make moves. Last time I left you in charge, these stupid men of ours fell out."

Tiffany pushed her cousin and said, "That shit was not my fault. They were like two little girls who buckled under pressure and took the shit out on each other. With all these other men in the house, they took it out on each other."

Cito came up behind them and said, "Well, I see half my house is back in order."

They both hugged him and said, "Old man, let me find out you still mastering the art of sneaking up on someone."

Cito laughed, "Ain't nothing old over here, I still got everything I had when I was your age, and more."

Tiffany laughed and said, "Cito, now you know that was too much information for us. Save that for your way too young chick, Sunshine."

"Yeah Cito, when are you going to settle down with someone your age?"

"What the hell I want with someone my age? They ain't on my level, most of them won't be able to keep up with me. I am a beast, I'm telling ya'll."

They both frowned, shook their heads and took off down the hall. Cito's louder than life laugh, yelled behind them asking them, "Where y'all going?"

They just waved him off and kept moving. Behind closed doors they had a lot of catching up to do. Diamond filled Tiffany in on what happen at Nina's house. Tiffany could not believe that Nina had actually let Diamond live especially after just close to a year ago, she tried to stomp her baby out of her. Even more amazing, Diamond let Nina live.

"OK, well here is the million dollar question, why didn't

you kill her when you killed Shamel?"

"Don't think I ain't think about it Tiff, after the history we had with that trick. And believe me, we ain't friends or nothing close to it, but she could have done me just as dirty as she did her sister, but she didn't for whatever reason. She could have let Ish kill me and my baby, but for whatever reason she didn't let that go down either, and she trusted me to let her live another day, so I had to respect that. Now don't get me wrong she deserves to die, but I couldn't be the one to do it. I thought for sure Tree would have, but she informed him of who was coming to her house and that gave him the upper hand to find out all the players in this take down.

The way she explained it, this whole shit ain't got nothing to do with the FBI. These are some dirty agents that want a piece of the rock and are willing to let Ish work for them and break them off to get it. Nina explained that Ish doesn't even know about the other three guys that Oarlock has involved, nor does he know that the Feds will not be there."

"Well how does Nina know all this?"

Diamond smiled with a sinister grin and said get this, "She's fucking all of them—Ish, Shamel and Oarlock."

"Get the fuck out of here...no she's not!"

"If I'm lying Tiff, shoot me down. I am telling you that is how I was able to kill Shahmel. I ain't go in right when she wanted me to, I at least let him get a few strokes in for the last time and right when I heard this nigga sounding like he was about to nut up, I burst in the room. When he rolled to get his gun, I shot his ass right in the middle of the forehead."

Tiffany thought the story was hilarious. "I know she was shook and mad too because she actually had to fuck that nigga."

"Shit, she's been fucking them and yeah she told me to try

to get him before he got in the pussy because she didn't want his grimy ass on her, but shit, you know me."

While they were packing up the last of the babies stuff Von appeared at the door. Both girls stopped talking. Tiffany gathered Kennedy's belonging and told Diamond she would see her downstairs in a few. She hugged Von and left them alone to talk.

G STREET CHRONICLES
A NEW URBAN DYNASTY

WWW.GSTREETCHRONICLES.COM

Chapter THIRTY-TWO

Nina's nerves were bad as hell. *What if the plan Tree had to pass Shamel off as being Diamond and her baby in the room didn't work? What if they turned the light on and realized the truth?* Oarlock and his three partners arrived at the same time. Nina played hostess hoping they would be so into their meeting and drinks they would stay away from that fucking room. So far things were going good, but her phone rang. She looked at the ID, it was Ish. *Fuck, now what?* Nina went into her room and answered the phone.

"Hello?"

"What's up baby, it's me. How are things going there?"

"Everything is fine, so far so good."

"Yo ma, has Shamel been down there?"

"He was here earlier and left to go see some chick he said, but he left his phone here in the living room."

"Oh OK, that would explain why that nigga ain't answering my phone calls. Look, in about three hours, some of Shamel boys from NY will be coming through to get ready for tomorrow, so make them as comfortable as possible."

As Nina listened to Ish talk she was thinking, *oh great, this is just what I need even more heat*. "Ish, do you think it's best for all them niggas to be camped out here? What if Oarlock comes by looking for you or something, sees them here, and you ain't tell him that you called in your own crew? You're going to get us all killed."

Ish thought about it for a minute and said, "You might be right baby. Let me make a few calls."

"Ish, when are you coming to see me? I mean damn, you been so wrapped up in this meeting and getting this money, that you've forgotten about home."

"Yo, when this is all over it will be all about you and me, but right now I can't cloud my head. I need to remain fully focused because any little mistakes will lead to this shit being deadly and me being on that end of it. I intend to be the one who walks out of there leaving the bodies of Cito, Von, Tree and Oarlock…but not me, baby."

Nina knew Ish was lying about how his time was being spent. She also knew that some bodies were going to drop tomorrow and Ish was sure to be one of them. "Fine Ish, do you. Look I got to run to the store. I'm hungry and y'all done had me cooped up in this house babysitting Diamond's ass."

"I know baby. You don't have to worry about that because later tonight, Shamel's going to take care of that little problem."

"OK, well I love you Ish. Be careful and I will see you tomorrow when it's over. Oh yeah, I got the plane tickets you asked me to get and we leave Monday morning at 7:30 for the Turks."

"Good baby, thanks."

Nina said her goodbyes and again told Ish she loved him for everything he had done for her. Had he not been in such a rush to get off the phone and back to Autumn, he would have read between the lines. Yeah, Nina had bought a plane ticket but just for herself. She went back into the living room area to make sure Oarlock and his people were OK and then back to her room to make a call to Tree.

After filling Tree in with the information she got from Ish and the information she had overheard from Oarlock, she made sure that everything she needed was packed and ready for her redeye flight out tonight. She was not playing the fool, she was getting gone before the smoke had a chance to get started and definitely before it cleared.

While sitting on her bed with her back to the door, she heard Oarlock come in the room. "Hey sexy, a dollar for your thoughts."

"Nothing much. I was just hoping that everything goes as planned and that you will come back to me safe and sound."

Oarlock kissed her on her forehead. "That's sweet. Anyway, we are about to be out. It's only a couple of hours before the meeting, and I want to make sure we have our stuff laid out in the warehouse to our advantage. But I am going to walk them out and come right back so you can show me how much you care before I leave."

Nina could not believe her luck, now she would have to fuck him too. "OK baby, I'll be right here waiting for you." When she heard the door shut she ran to the front to make sure he was not still in the house, then hurriedly called the state police chief with a three-way to the local FBI top brass. As soon as she got them both on the phone she talked fast while watching Oarlock from the window.

"Look, my name is Nina Whitehead, and I don't have long, so please listen. State FBI Agent, Brian Oarlock, is in a partnership with three other agents who have partnered with a drug dealer by the name of Ishmel Jennings. There is to be a big drug meeting and a change of hands deal going down in the morning at 5:00, in the old fabric warehouse downtown. I have to go."

With that Nina hung up, dialed a random number and hung up, just in case Oarlock hit the redial button. When Oarlock came back inside he went directly to Nina's room and undressed. The sight of his old, clammy, overweight, body made her want to throw up. Nina was also getting undressed, but before she could even get her mind right to pretend she would enjoy this fat fucker humping and sweating on her with his ugly, uncircumcised dick, she needed to first get high. She laid out four lines of cocaine on a glass tray and rolled up a hundred dollar bill because she felt she deserved to snort from big money. Since all this shit started, Nina had picked up a habit that Oarlock was happy to supply from drugs they confiscated from busts. As a result, she was always on the best of the best. After taking two hits she passed the tray to Oarlock, who gladly hit the remaining two lines. Once Nina got into the zone, she fucked Oarlock like she never had before and like he had never been fucked before. She was so zoned that she never heard Ish come into the door.

* * *

Tree arrived at Cito's house for the meeting and walked right pass Von like he was not even there. Tiffany and Diamond had been back for awhile after dropping the babies off with their mothers at the airport. Von extended his hand to Tree but he moved his arm before Von made contact.

"Look man, what happened was all out of frustration and anger. You know you are like a brother to me and I would never let harm come to you. I will admit that I was jealous a bit because you had your family and had protected them, while I slipped on my pimping. And, no, that ain't no reason for the shit I said, but we are family and we've been though a lot. Sorry don't fix the shit I said and did, but on everything I love man, I ain't mean none of that shit."

Tree really wanted to make peace with Von, but he just kept thinking what his mother always says, 'what a drunk man says is usually what he means'. And even if Von ain't mean everything he said, some of the shit he really did mean and it had been on his chest for awhile. Look Von, I told you, in battle I got you for the sake of La Familia but I can't shake that some of what you said was on your heart for awhile, and it was truly what you meant. Von looked at the floor defeated.

Tree grabbed Tiffany's hand and walked towards the conference room where the meeting was to take place.

Diamond rubbed Von's back and whispered in his ear, "Just give Tree some time."

Von said, "Fuck it I tried. At the end of the day, Von going to do Von with or without him."

Diamond said, "Look at you, the same shit that started this is what you're doing now. What is really going on with you?"

"With me? What the fuck? You're supposed to be my fucking wife, and you're questioning me about some shit I did to another man? How you looking D?"

"I'm looking like the voice of reason Von. We're a fucking family and never has your anger showed like this. So again, what the fuck is up?"

"Ok D, this shit about giving up the game was the idea of you and Tree...I ain't ready. If anything, I'm suppose to be the man once Cito retires not some other street corner nigga."

"Nigga, you're damn right, it was me but not Tree. I asked you to get out for us. But if that ain't what you want, then at this meeting by all means, speak your fucking mind since you've been on a roll all this time. And like Tree, I will ride with you on this take down in the morning, but after that I'm out. Take it how you want but because of your status in these streets, niggas touched your family. Do you realize that they kidnapped me and your daughter? If Nina didn't have an ounce of heart I would be dead and so would your daughter. But if none of this means shit to you, cool but I'm out, I'm done."

Von responded harshly, "Oh, now you're out? The same big mouth that claimed to be a rider with me, and now you're out? Well fine D, be out. I'm sick of motherfuckers turning their backs on me. I don't need anyone and I'm damn sure going to be alright."

By the time he finished his sentence, Diamond squared off at him and began fighting him like a bitch on the streets, screaming, "You want to act like a bitch, nigga, I'm going to show you about being a bitch."

When Von got his composure he raised his hand to punch Diamond, but then put it down slowly when he felt that cold steel pointed in the back of his head. "I know stress will kill a motherfucker, but if you hit her you will not have to worry about stress killing you. Now the meeting is getting started and I suggest that you go in there, play your position and cool the fuck down. Y'all as a family will fix all this at a later date. Right now, all of y'all are turning your anger towards the wrong people. They're expecting everyone to fall apart here. You have stressed my man out and made him feel like he has lost his position. And oh, man, you know I can't have that happen. He is the king till he dies, even once he retires. So now, please go into the meeting because we surely would not want you to be late and miss out on anything because after all, you are the third piece to this triangle of a family Cito put together. You do remember that symbol you wear around your neck don't you?"

Von looked down to his iced out triangle with each of their initials on a part of the three sides. He looked at Sunshine then Diamond and walked in the direction of the conference room. Sunshine helped Diamond straighten her clothes, pointed towards the conference room and walked in the opposite direction. Diamond was at a loss. Someone had surely forgotten to tell her that Cito had a thug trick.

Chapter THIRTY-THREE

Autumn went to visit Lil Mike at the hospital. When she walked into the room he was sitting up watching the game. She was smiling from ear to ear, happy to see her baby doing better.

"Hey baby, how long you been up?"

"Long enough to know your sexy ass better had stopped at the restaurant, got me something to eat and made sure that everything is running smooth."

Autumn held the bag up she had behind her back. Mike called her over closer to him pretending he was about to kiss her and grabbed the bag.

"Man you're dirty as hell."

Mike laughed and kissed her. "Sit down sexy, tell me what's good in them streets and why my sister punk ass has not been up here."

Autumn filled him in on the kidnapping, the meeting and how Diamond made it back home. Mike quickly lost his appetite.

"Look baby mamma, I need to get the fuck up out this hospital. The drop is going down in the morning, and I need to make sure I'm there for the family."

Autumn pondered this for a while, then asked, "Just how do you think I'm suppose to get you out of here before the doctor releases you?"

Mike smiled at her and she was like putty, because his smile usually got him anything he wanted from her. "Give me your phone." Mike called Kesahn, and after a brief conversation he asked Autumn to help him get dressed.

Autumn asked, "Well how about I help you undress first? I'll be sure to be gentle."

Mike pulled her towards him, she slipped off her Cole Haan's and slowly took off her Michael Kors' jumpsuit. Mike's dick instantly stood at attention, just looking at her caramel smooth skin.

"Baby, go lock the door." She locked the door, crawled on the bed and pulled the covers back saying, "I see someone is happy to see me."

"Yeah, he is. Why don't you give him a kiss?"

Autumn proceeded to kiss down Mike's body until she got to his rock hard dick. Taking him into her mouth slowly, she decided to show him just how much she had missed him. She could feel the veins in his dick and knew he was close to cuming, but she wanted to feel him inside her. She slowly crawled on top of him being careful not to hurt him because he was still recovering from bullet wounds. Autumn and Mike became one and she rode him just like he always liked it. She always started out facing him and managed to turn around on his dick and let him slap that ass while she brought him to a hard nut. Once Mike had cum he was ready for a nap. Autumn got up, washed them both off, helped him get dressed and wheeled him downstairs where Kesahn was waiting.

"What it do my nigga? It's about time you got your punk-ass up out that hospital bed and got back to work. Nigga get shot and want to feel like he's entitled to take a vacation, when he needs to be putting in work."

Mike laughed because he knew his boy was just glad he was OK but was to thugged to say it.

"Yeah, well my baby got me right up there in the room so now I'm ready."

"Y'all some nasty mothers, up in the hospital fucking with all them sick people up in there."

"Don't be mad because you ain't never had the experience of fucking in a hospital bed."

"If you were not all hurt up I would punch you, but being the frail nigga you are, I will save it for later."

"OK, well enough of the emotional talk, we need to get to the La Familia meeting so we'll know what's going on for the morning." Kesahn asked his friend, "You think you're ready to be going to battle after just getting out the hospital?"

"Man I am fine."

Kesahn proceeded to Cito's house for the meeting.

G STREET CHRONICLES
A NEW URBAN DYNASTY

WWW.GSTREETCHRONICLES.COM

Chapter THIRTY-FOUR

Nina was in shock. There she was riding the dick of this cop that was supposed to be Ish's partner. Ish was furious and had pulled his gun before he even knew it. Oarlock had a smile on his face and lifted Nina up off him.

"Ishmel, you need to calm down…it's not that serious."

Oarlock rolled over to the side of the bed, but Ish still had his gun drawn on him.

"So what now Ishmel? You're going to kill an FBI agent?"

Ish tilted his head to the side and looked at both of them with red eyes. With one swift move he reached out and snatched Nina by the neck and was in her face. "So that is why all the questions of when I was coming over, and what I was doing because you was fucking this fat fucker right here?"

Nina was still a little high and this point she was just tired of the drama. If she was going to die she just wanted to get it over with. Nina spit at him and said, "So what, you can fuck that pretty broad with the long brown hair in Maryland, and

I can't get my grove on? Shit, truth be told, I was doing a favor for you by keeping that fat, nasty, greasy, fucker happy till the meeting took place because he was getting impatient with your ass. Shit, he was keeping me high and as instructed by you, I was making sure everyone was not getting antsy because you were so busy playing the man before you become the man, and wining and dining that trick. Shit, your own brother was ready to head back to NY. Oh yeah, I've been fucking him too!

You're hurting my fucking neck, so I would appreciate it if you let go of me right damn now!"

Ish could not believe this trick was trying him. *Just who the fuck did she think she was talking to?* Ish let her go and she walked over to the dresser and prepped another two lines. She turned to Ish and said, "Wait a few minutes because I have some more to tell you. Since you're about to be the king and all, and I'm pretty sure I will not be around to see it, I at least want you to know everything."

"Hell, Ish, you owe me that."

She looked at Oarlock and said, "As for you, get your funky, limp dick out of my bed."

Oarlock walked towards her and without even looking, she turned from the first line she had hit and pointed a gun in his face. "I wish your ass would give me a reason to blow you the fuck all over this place. Remember those hollow points you gave me as a gift? Well hell, why not share the gift with you? Now give me a reason agent!"

Oarlock backed up and grabbed his pants. Looking at Ish, it seemed they both had the same thought. . .*either the shit she was snorting was that good or she was really just ready to die.* Either way, Ish did not take his gun off of either of them, but had grabbed Oarlock's gun in the event he got a case of itchy fingers. Nina didn't even bother to get dressed, she was just killing time. She had a good feeling that Ish would eventually show up especially since he had not heard from his brother. Nina sat down in the chair in front of the window and crossed her legs. She was so high she felt no fear.

G STREET CHRONICLES
~A NEW URBAN DYNASTY~

WWW.GSTREETCHRONICLES.COM

Chapter THIRTY-FIVE

Cito made sure that everyone knew their position and what was suppose to take place. Tree had called Cito earlier and informed him of the conversation he had with Nina. Cito had already gotten a call from the chief of police and from someone at FBI about the call that came in from Nina. Right after, Cito had Sunshine buy tickets for Von and Tree to get out of the states within the next couple of hours, with the agreement that they would be gone for a period of no less then three months. Tiffany sat in the meeting shaking her head because this was so unreal. After everything, they were now asking her to be away from her husband and him away from his family for three months.

"With all do respect Cito, how can they just up and leave their families? We just had babies and now you want us to be here while our husbands are gone?"

Cito said, "It is either that or they will be under the watchful eyes of the law and possibly spend time in jail."

Tiffany didn't say another word.

"Now in about thirty minutes, you all need to be suited

up in your vest and ready to roll. There will be no drop in the morning, it is too hot to even play it that route. All the other families that were to attend the meeting have been informed. Make this clean and let's all come home in one piece. I would like to say there are no sides here to take, but the family side. La Familia is what it has always been, a strong structured foundation. We have had a few problems, but that never held us down from being who we are. If there is anyone who feels they would like to back out now or want no parts, then speak now."

Just then Lil Mike stepped in. Cito said, "You're late, sit down."

Mike and Kesahn did as they were told.

"Next order of business, now that the late comers found it in their hearts to join us, there is a change in who is taking over the spots that Von and Tree once held in the streets. I made the decision, so if anyone has a problem with it, I don't really give a shit. I am old, I am tired and I am handling this shit. I gave you youngsters some power and you couldn't handle it."

Tree and Von looked at each other and then at Cito because this was the first that they heard of him choosing replacements.

Cito lit a cigar and sat back in his chair. He then addressed Tiffany and Diamond. "Do I have to dismiss you two before I make the announcement?"

Both of them shook their heads, no.

"OK. Any outbursts and I am going to be pissed. Now back to business. This is why I don't have females in meetings, they distract me and they are so emotional."

Tree was getting impatient with Cito.

"Enough!!"

"The new chiefs-in-charge and the people you will be reporting to are Kesahn and Mike."

Tiffany lost her balance and Tree had to help her up off the floor. Diamond had a wicked grin on her face, happy that her cousin would reign chief of the streets. Tiffany was the only one that didn't know he had been groomed for this day. He was Von's choice to replace him when Tree chose Ish. Tree held Tiffany in his lap to keep her from speaking. Kesahn and Mike stood up and shook Cito's hand. Cito then handed them chains with iced out triangles on them. He officially welcomed them to the Family. Everyone congratulated them and slapped fives. Tiffany still did not say a word but she did search Tree's eyes. He knew he was busted so he looked away.

He whispered in her ear, "Baby be happy for your brother. He is smart and he has been well groomed. If Cito didn't feel he could handle it, he would not have chosen him. Mike knows the game ain't forever. The good thing is you gave him the restaurant so he has an established front. He will not be on the corner."

Tiffany prayed he was right. She finally got up enough energy to stand and went over to congratulate her brother. Just before she left Tree, he said one more thing. "Baby, Mike was shot when there was a shooting at the restaurant. I didn't tell you because it was around the same time Diamond was kidnapped, and I knew if I told you that you would try to leave the house and go to the hospital."

Tiffany bent over and said, "You're late, your father already filled me in while you and Von were having a PMS moment."

Tree slapped her on her ass and told her to go congratulate her brother. He walked out the room giving Kesahn a pound and went to get dressed. It was now time to roll out.

Von walked into Tree's room and said, "Man, no matter what, we're brothers till we die. I know you ain't feeling me right now and I probably would be the same way, so I get it. Anyway, now this is business. We need to call Ish and make some communication with him before he suspects something is wrong."

Tree agreed with him and called Ish. "Yo nigga, what it do? You ready to become the king?"

Ish smiled at the thought of that and the fact that Tree had no idea what was in store for his ass. "Yeah man, I'm just trying to wrap my mind around this shit for real."

"So nigga, we going to go have drinks to celebrate the end of my reign and the beginning of yours, or what?"

"Man Tree, I'm boo'd up right now with my girl, so I ain't going to be able to make it and be at the spot in a few hours."

"Man, I understand. Well let's get together after the drop."

"Cool, that's what's up. We can differently do that, my treat. Yo, where Von at?"

"He's right here, man."

"Any word on his wife and kid?"

"Same old same, Ish. No word yet on Diamond or the baby. But yo, let me hit you right back, that nigga, Cito is calling."

"Yeah OK, cool, but make sure you call to let me know what happened with Diamond."

"Will do."

Tree hung up and said to Von, "Well, there it is…he still doesn't know Diamond is home. Let's roll out."

Autumn, Tiffany, Diamond and surprisingly Sunshine were all suited up. Von was really having a problem with them rolling out, but they were suppose to be outside keeping eyes on anything suspicious while they went in to handle Ish.

Cito and Monty lead the way out. It had been a long time since Cito had to get his hands dirty and the first time a lot of them in the crew had ever seen him in this form.

Chapter THIRTY-SIX

Ish picked up his cell and saw Tree's number and laughed at the thought that that nigga was getting ready to die or go to jail. He was sick of playing like they were cool and was ready to get this over with but he played his part while talking to Tree.

When he got off the phone he called his NY connect. He was still worried because he hadn't heard from his brother. Nina was still naked and getting high while Ish was holding his gun on her and Oarlock.

He instructed his crew, "Meet me at her house right now. The door is unlocked."

"Guess this just ain't your fucking day huh, fat ass?" Nina said to Oarlock.

"Shut your whore ass up and just kill yourself because I'm tired of looking at you," Oarlock snapped.

Nina looked at the clock and thought, *well let the games begin*. She knew that Ish's people were not far and Tree and his crew should not be that far either. Funny thing was she saw Oarlock messing with his pocket and knew he was trying to call his people on his phone. Didn't matter, maybe they will just kill each other.

When Tree and the crew arrived they parked around back and then set up on the sides of the house and on the roof. Nina had already told them Oarlock had three working with him, and Ish had a crew of five minus his brother, since he was dead.

Oarlock's people could hear the conversation going on and knew he was in some shit. They decided to head back to Nina's and find out what the fuck was going on. This was payday, they could not afford any fuck ups.

Tree radioed into the crew that they were going into the house so watch out for anybody approaching. Shoot to kill, was Tree's instructions. Cito, Monty, Tree and Von, all got to the door and spoke words with their eyes. Tree turned the knob and the door opened. They walked in slowly, following the faint voices. Once they got to the doorway of the room, they all drew their guns.

Ish was in shock when he noticed who had just come in. Von walked up to Ish and told him to drop his gun nice and slow. Ish did as he was told and then tried to play them.

"Man, I aint want to get y'all involved. After I found out this bitch was alive and working with the Feds, I watched till it was a perfect time to catch her and this fat pig and kill them."

Nina bust out laughing, leaned over and took another hit. Cito laughed too and said to Ish, "When my son brought you in I didn't like you, but I tried to respect his decision."

Oarlock moved a little too sudden for Cito and he shot him in the leg. "Please be still Brian, you know I hate sudden movement. You have known me long enough to know I just hate that."

Oarlock was screaming out in pain. Cito said, "Brian, I

am talking and if you can't keep your mouth shut with all that damn screaming, I will have to help you with it."

Brian Oarlock did his best to be quiet because he knew Cito was a man of his word.

"Anyway, back to you Ish. I never liked you and to think he was giving you the world but you wanted more."

Tree told Nina to get dressed. She got up and did as she was told. Once she was dressed, she turned to Ish and said, "By the way, the reason that you have not heard from your brother is because right before he got that final nut off, Diamond shot his ass. He's in the same tomb of a room you planted for her."

Ish was outraged and jumped up to go after her. Tree waved his gun at him and said, "Sit your happy ass down."

Just then someone came through the door. Von was covering the front room and since no gun fire could be heard, Cito and Tree knew it had to be one of them.

Cito continued to talk. "You know Ishmel, I never like a liar, and you boy, you're a liar.

Autumn walked in the room, Ish stood up and said "Baby, what are you doing here?"

Von smiled and said, "Well maybe we should introduce you. This here is my little sister."

Ish was dumbfounded. "Your what?"

"My little sister, and you know Lil Mike don't you? Well, she's his wifey. Now you ain't think you could pull no honey like her with just money and talk did you?"

Ish was pissed. This whole time he had been played by all of them and here he was thinking he was playing them. He sat down and prayed that his crew was on their way. Just then they heard gun shots. Von and Tree ran for the front door. Cito shot Oarlock and before he could turn the gun on Ish,

Ish had seized his gun off the floor and shot Cito in the arm and hit Nina in the forehead. She was so high she probably didn't even feel the pain.

Autumn ran while shooting at Ish with her gun. Ish was determined he was not going out without a fight.

Tree and Von entered the hallway with bullets flying everywhere. They shot off a couple at Ish's boys and then ducked in one of the rooms. They continued to trade gun fire, room to room, no one taking any chances on entering the hallway. Knowing they needed to get out of that room alive to protect their family, Tree and Von devised a plan to climb out the window.

Autumn was able to hit Ish in the shoulder before he caught her in the calf. Autumn was down, and Ish stood over her and grabbed her by her hair. He was pissed and ready to take back control of the situation. Knowing he couldn't go out the front door, he drug her to a window on the side of the house, opened it and threw Autumn out before jumping out himself. Sunshine saw the commotion going on by the side window and called it to Diamond and Tiffany's attention. They looked over and saw Ish dragging Autumn by her hair. They all jumped out the car and ran towards him. Ish was firing off rounds at them and then turned his gun on Autumn. They were all standing in the driveway which led to the back of the house and Ish was determined he was going to leave that driveway and kill all those bitches in the process.

Autumn stood up as best she could and decided she would die before she let Ish kill Diamond or Tiffany.

"Autumn, you dirty bitch, are you ready to meet your maker?"

"Sure Ish, as long as you know you're going with me." Ish raised his gun to shoot her in the head and the girls raised theirs at the same time. Suddenly a shot went off and they froze because Autumn was still standing. Sunshine ran toward Cito who had sent off the fatal bullet from behind them. Autumn was still frozen in her spot. Diamond ran and grabbed her and helped her to the car. Sunshine saw that Cito was hit and wrapped her head band around his arm to stop the bleeding.

"Where is Monty, Cito?"

"He was with the boys when the shooting started. I need to go back in."

Sunshine did not argue with him but thought it best that they go in from the front since most of the shooting was coming from the back.

Hearing the gunfire on the opposite side of the house when Tree and Von fell to the ground they both got up and ran toward the shots. They reached the front of the house at the same time as Cito and Sunshine. They all saw a car stop slightly past the driveway and three men jumped out of it hurrying back toward the house. Cito chirped Mike and asked his location.

"We're on the roof."

"Look down and tell me what you see."

"We got you."

Mike and Kesahn let off a round of shots and laid every last one of Oarlock's men out. They saw two dudes coming out of the house limping, trying to get to their car. Kesahn waited until they got in the car, aimed at the gas tank and fired. The car blew up.

Kesahn high-fived Mike and said, "Now that is how you take a person out. Nice, sweet, and smooth, no chaser."

"Yo K, you're a sick man, son."

Cito was chirping Monty, but getting no answer. He heard

rapid gunfire that suddenly stopped. He knew there were three more of Ish's people inside and he needed to go in and make sure his people were OK. He made his way in the front door and heard a couple of moans coming from the upstairs hallway. He had both of his guns drawn and ready to fire. Cito walked up on a couple of his workers who had been shot and killed. Upstairs he found Monty, who had been shot and was not looking good. He bent down to help him and one of the New York cats walked up on him and shot him in the head.

Monty cried out and the dude smiled and said, "Let me introduce myself pimp. My name is Treysure. Ish had me come down to help him out, but you know he was never really cut out for the game, so I am sure he's dead right about now. So with your boy gone, that leaves me to take over because hey, New York niggas are the craziest." Treysure lifted his gun and shot Monty.

Sunshine had just reached the hallway and saw what happen. With tears in her eyes, she snuck up on Treysure and slit his throat.

Tree and Von checked on their wives, forced them to get back in the car and headed inside to find Cito. They were running up the stairs and stopped dead in their tracks when they saw their father, their mentor, dead in the floor and Sunshine in the floor rocking his body. Tree walked over, picked her up from the floor and carried her outside. Von chirped Diamond to bring the car around. When she pulled up, Tree put Sunshine in the car.

"Leave right now and don't stop till you've made it back to the house."

Tiffany kept asking what was going on and no one would answer.

Von yelled, "Pull off now and call the doc to come out to the house to check on anyone that might come back injured."

Von and Tree walked back towards the house. They motioned Mike and Kesahn to come down.

Chapter THIRTY-SEVEN

Sunshine had not said a word on the ride back, she had completely spaced out on them. Diamond was wondering why Tree and Von came out the building but Cito and Monty did not. She knew her cousin was on the roof, the safest place he could be. That had been one of Cito's instructions that he was to stay on the roof and hit anything moving. Tiffany noticed that Sunshine had a lot of blood on her clothes and was wondering if she had been hit. When they got back to the house Sunshine still could not get herself together enough to get out the car. Tiffany helped Autumn get out and then went back to help Diamond with Sunshine. Once they got her in the house they asked her where Cito was.

Sunshine begin to rock back and forth holding her stomach and spoke for the first time ever, "Cito was going to be a dad."

Autumn looked at her and said, "Bitch what you mean was going to, where is Cito?"

"He's dead. They shot him like a pig in the head. Both Cito and Monty are dead"

Everyone began to cry. What the hell had gone wrong? How did someone get that close to Cito? Doc arrived and tended to Autumn's wounds and everyone else who came in, one by one. Tiffany was starting to get worried because Tree and Von had not made it back yet.

* * *

Von and Tree got in the van, changed their clothes and got their bags ready. Tree felt bad that he had not told Tiffany that he would not be coming back to the house, but going straight to the airport. Earlier that morning they had two people pose as them and take a flight over to Cancun. The plan was to have a paper trail to show they were not in the states when the shooting took place. They had Cito's jet waiting for them to take them to Cancun and bring the other two people back. Mike and Kesahn dropped them off at the jet strip and told them to call when they got there.

Before getting on the plane Von turned to Tree and asked "So what now, man?"

Tree shrugged his shoulders and said, "I don't know but like I said before, I'm out."

When they get back, he was no longer going to be in the life. Tree took his chain off, handed it to Von and boarded the plane. Mike shook his head, got back in the car and drove off.

Kesahn finally spoke and said, "So with Cito gone, I guess us talking over this shit is a wash."

Mike shrugged his shoulders and said, "One or both of them niggas need to take the time and get their minds right, then come back and take over."

"Yo, did you not hear that nigga, Tree, say he's out?"

"Yeah, I heard him but, whatever…you never fully get

out the game."

When they got back to the house Tiffany lost it. "Where is Tree and Von, why aren't they with you?"

"Tiff, after everything went down they left the states.," Mike explained, "that is what they were instructed to do, and people had already flown over this morning as their decoy."

Diamond asked, "So no good bye, no nothing?"

"Look y'all know what it is, don't stress me. Shit is falling apart and y'all just thinking about yourselves"

Mike walked off went to check on Autumn. A couple of days later, Tiffany got a call but when she said hello no one would say anything. She started to hang up but just held the phone and listened to the person breathing because she knew it was her husband. Diamond was walking around being the backbone for everyone. No one had left Cito's house in over a week. Police had come by a couple of times with a few questions. Diamond was the spokesperson and basically acted socked whenever police revealed any information or asked a question. Diamond explained to the police that Tree and Von had gone to Mexico overseeing some building on a property they had invested in. She gave them the name of the other parties in the investment and their contact numbers. Cito had a lot of connections and all the bases were covered. Police thought it kind of strange that they flew out the morning of the shootout, but with everything checking out they just wrote the shooting off as a drug deal gone bad with some dirty agents. Police did have one question about the whereabouts of Cito's right hand man and lieutenant, Monty. Diamond stated that he was with Cito the day they left going to dinner. Sunshine was sitting in the corner looking spaced-out and Tiffany quickly handed her Kennedy to throw the cops off from reading her.

When the police finally left, Diamond turned to Sunshine and said, "I thought you said Monty was dead too."

"He was, I saw him laying there right under Cito, and I saw the guy shoot him before I cut his throat."

Diamond called Kesahn and gave him the information about Monty's body not being found. Kesahn said he would make a few calls and get back to her. They still had not laid Cito to rest, that was to be done in a couple of days. They were not sure if Von and Tree would fly back or not.

Chapter THIRTY-EIGHT

Monty made it out of the building but he was badly shot up. Luckily he had on his vest or that last shot would have killed him. He could not believe that Cito was dead. This was hurting him to his heart. Monty had been shacked up in an apartment for about two weeks nursing his wounds and drinking himself in and out of consciousness. What was his life going to be like without Cito? He didn't know anything else but this life. He could take over Cito's spot because he knew it just as well as he did and knew all the connections and partners, but it would not be the same. Monty could not even bring himself to go back to the house after having his cousin's dead body laying on him and looking into his eyes. Cito died for his boys and for honor.

Every night Tiffany got the same call with just breathing, she would just talk knowing he would not respond back. She told him that they would be laying Cito to rest in a couple of days and the police did not come across Monty's body, so some how or another he made it out alive but no one knows where he is. Tiffany would update him on their daughter and what was going on with her. She would always end the call telling him she loved him and would see him in Georgia.

Diamond was noticing that her cousin was sleeping a lot and would get sick right after eating. She wrote it off as it being her nerves because of everything that happened and her missing Tree.

They had buried Cito two months ago and still got no word from Monty. Sunshine was starting to show now and it was taking everything they had to keep her spirits up. Diamond constantly reminded her that her actions would get her ass kicked by Cito for acting weak. Sunshine usually smiled at the thought of that.

Tiffany was out on the patio reading a book when Diamond came and sat beside her. "Hey Tiff, what's good?"

"Nothing, just sitting here really passing time. I'm probably going to fly out Friday, check on the house in Georgia, and see what the decorator has done. As soon as the house is finished I'll be leaving to go there, as Tree has asked me to. It's over, but a part of me feels like I should wait here for him."

"Well Tiff, if your husband asked you to leave this place, then you need to respect it and leave as soon as the house is officially finished and ready to move in."

"What about you D? I just can't leave you here."

"I'm a big girl and I won't be too far behind you. Mike and Kesahn have been real good at keeping the money rolling in and the blocks busy, and I have a meeting scheduled to introduce them to the other partners who Cito worked with. After that, they will officially take over Cito's chair until Tree and Von make a decision on what is to happen next."

"Well, I guess Von will be making the decision because you know Tree is out."

"Yeah Tiff, I hear you, and Von supposed to be out too but the game has changed. Cito was not supposed to die. Anyway Tiff, let me ask you this, when was the last time you had a period?"

Tiffany thought for awhile and said, "To be honest, I can't remember."

"Well Tiff, are you feeling OK?"

"Yeah, I'm fine. You know my nerves are still bad and I miss my man like hell."

"Well then, you won't mind at all taking this."

"Bitch, you're crazy, my husband has been gone for almost three months now."

"OK, and for about that same amount of time your ass has been sick. Oh, did you forget that night you spent with your husband before everything went down?"

Tiffany thought back and Diamond was right, they had had sex that night. She snatched the box and said, "I will take it just to ease your mind, and prove I ain't pregnant."

"OK big shot, go on in there and handle your business. Call me when you're done, I'm going to check on bad and badder."

Kennedy and Keyetta had bonded so tightly they would not go to sleep unless they were in the same room. Diamond did not know what they were going to do when the baby's were separated when Tiffany moved to Georgia. After making sure the babies were sleeping and checking on Sunshine, Diamond went downstairs to see what Tiffany's test results were. When she knocked on the door, Tiffany didn't answer so she walked in. Tiffany was sitting on the countertop and threw the test at Diamond. She caught it, looked at the window and said, "Told you. Tree has knocked you up again. I'll be damn. Make sure this one is a boy."

Tiffany laughed. "Shut up! Well, I guess once I get to Georgia, I need to start looking for a nanny right away, because girl you know good and well I can't handle two of them so close in age. Look at Kennedy and Kenyetta, I'm ready to tear my hair out with those two."

Diamond hugged Tiffany. "Good thing we're going to be neighbors so I can help you."

Chapter THIRTY-NINE

Von and Tree did not speak a lot the first couple of weeks they were in Mexico. Eventually they did exchange words here and there. Von apologized to Tree every chance he got. Tree knew he could not be mad at him forever but he was not ready to forgive him. He continued to call and just listen to Tiffany ramble on about everything that was going on at home. His happiest moment was when he found out she was pregnant again. The investment property was almost finished and the investors would be leaving soon. Tree was happy because he was tired of fronting like he was away on business. He did tell Von what Tiffany mentioned about Monty's body not being found at the scene and no one hearing from him. Von was shocked but was hoping that he would show face in due time because he had promised his wife that he would not stay in the game. He knew Tree was serious about being out and that left him next in line.

They were sitting in the dinning room area when someone knocked at the door. Tree just assumed it was room service because they had ordered about an hour ago. Tree answered the door and stood frozen in his spot. Monty reached out and hugged Tree. He was gone so long, Von went to see what the problem was. When Von saw Monty he said, "Man, where the fuck you been? Got niggas stressing and shit, and look at you."

Monty stepped in and told them all about where he had been. They both noticed he had a limp and rubbed his shoulder a lot. Von asked the question he was sure that Tree also wanted to know.

"So now what Monty? Are you going to take Cito's chair?"

I've been thinking about it long and hard while I was out of commission. "That is what he would have wanted. We fought side by side many days. I was just fucked up because I felt like I failed him. It should have been me that died. This was his kingdom, he started it, he was supposed to still be here."

Von and Tree understood where he was coming from and they had on many occasions felt the same way.

"Well I ain't come out here to stay too long because I got to get back and get to work. I'm sure everyone is just winging it and not sure what roll they're playing. I heard that Lil Mike and Kesahn have been holding it down well."

"Yo, Monty, Cito's finally going to be a father man."

"What the fuck you talking about Tree?"

"His top bitch, Sunshine, is pregnant. Diamond has been taking care of her ass and keeping a close eye on her. Before they buried him, Diamond made sure they took whatever they needed for DNA."

A dad and he ain't even fucking here to see it. I'll be damn, Cito still had it in him. I got to make sure to send Diamond something special too for holding shit down. Von you picked a real winner.

So being that y'all sharing an apartment am I to assume that y'all made up?"

Von looked at Tree and Tree looked down at the floor.

"Look both of y'all, I think of you just like Cito did, as my sons. Von, I ain't speak on it because Cito had it, but you were wrong and there ain't no way around it, but Tree, you know the nigga's real heart. Cito and I had a similar falling out. His wife was a girl I was trying to get with. I met her first and was trying to wife her, but he swept her off her feet faster then I could. We exchanged a few hateful words, but in the end we were family. We got pass it, and y'all saw how tight we were…nothing but death separated us."

Von and Tree understood where he was coming from and knew they needed to dead whatever was going on with them. Monty got up and said, "Well I must head back now. I'm sure there are going to be a lot of questions."

Tree and Von shook his hand and told him they would get up with him when they got back.

G STREET CHRONICLES
~A NEW URBAN DYNASTY~

WWW.GSTREETCHRONICLES.COM

Chapter FORTY

Tiffany finally moved into her new home in Georgia but was really missing her husband. This pregnancy was getting the best of her—the morning sickness, combined with being horny, was enough to make her scream. Kennedy was looking more and more like her father each day. Tiffany and Kennedy took daily walks to check on Diamond's house. She also made it a routine to check on Lil Mike everyday, because she still worried about him even though he was not technically in the streets. One thing she and Diamond were equally happy about was Monty was taking over Cito's spot which meant that their husbands could be out for good.

Tiffany put Kennedy down around 8:30, and took a hot bath while waiting for her nightly call from Tree. She was praying that maybe tonight he would let her hear his voice. It had been months now and she was lonely and emotional. Sitting in the tub Tiffany reminisced on her five years with Tree and everything they had been through, gained and lost.

She heard Kennedy crying. She hurried out the tub and threw on her robe. After getting the baby settled down she realized Tree had not called. She was tired, and decided to go to bed, but made sure she kept the phone near.

* * *

Tree wanted to surprise his wife so he did not tell anyone he was coming home. He was dropped off first and then the jet took Von to Maryland. Tree rented a car and headed toward his new home. When he walked in he was pleased with all the work Tiffany and the decorators had put into the house. He went into Kennedy's room first, picked up his baby girl and held her close. She had gotten so big and looked so much like him. After sitting with her for thirty minutes, he put her back in her crib and proceeded down the hall to his room.

He stood in the doorway staring at how beautiful his wife looked. Her pregnancy really gave her a glow. He went over to the bed, knelt down and whispered in Tiffany's ear, "I love you."

A smile came over her face but she didn't open her eyes. Tree talked to her a little longer and realized she must have thought she was dreaming. He got undressed and slid in bed with her. He kissed her softly on her neck and she started moving around. This dream was feeling a little too good to her. Tree then moved down to her toes and one at a time, just like she always liked, he took them into his mouth. She moaned softly as he began rubbing his hands up her legs, and that's when she woke up. When she saw that her husband was there in the flesh she was overcome with joy, crying hysterically.

"Baby, you're really home! It is you!"

Tiffany could not believe this was happening. Tree wiped away her tears and told her how much he missed and loved her. She held on to Tree all night not wanting to let him out of her sight. They made love over and over until they fell asleep. The next morning Tree let Tiffany sleep and checked on Kennedy. When he walked into her room she gave him a huge smile. Tree was so happy she knew who he was. He was so worried that when he walked into her room she would cry, seeing him as a stranger. Tree gave her a bath, got her dressed and fed her by the time Tiffany came downstairs.

Tree and Tiffany spent the day talking. He gave her the news about Monty taking over.

"I'm out but if Monty runs into a problem, I have no choice...that was the commitment I made when I was young. Cito let me out the game with no problems, but it is always written if you are called you have to go. It's like being in the military."

Tiffany understood, and hoped he would never be called.

G STREET CHRONICLES
~ A NEW URBAN DYNASTY ~

WWW.GSTREETCHRONICLES.COM

Chapter FORTY-ONE

Mike was loving his new job and was planning to ask Autumn to marry him. They had been kicking it for two years now and he wanted to be with her.

Monty had picked up where Cito left off so it made everyone's life a little better.

Kesahn was still the playboy he had always been.

Diamond and Von where packing to move because their home was finally ready. Mike promised he would be down to visit because he had to come see his sister especially after she gave birth to the new baby.

Sunshine had given birth to a boy and named him Cito Jr. Of course, Monty had a DNA test done and it was Cito's baby. So needless to say, Sunshine and the baby were set for life.

Things were getting back to as normal as possible. La Familia had been tried a couple of times by people that thought since Cito was dead and his sons were out of this business, they could take over, but Monty was on it. Monty sent Tree his medallion back when he found it in Cito's office. Von had brought it back with him. When Tree received it in the mail he smiled at the memories the medallion held and put it around his neck. Yeah, everything was going good with members of La Familia. Until that knock on the door…

Monty opened the door slowly after seeing the police on the other side. "What can I do for you?"

Monty was shocked as the police informed him that Sunshine had been killed and the baby was missing.

Tricyo born in new York City, raised in East Orange, New Jersey, attended parochial schools in east and south orange, New Jersey, is a graduate of University of Maryland Eastern Shore. She is the mother of an adorable two year old, and currently resides in Charlotte, NC.

Reading has always been a quiet time passion for her which sparked the inclination to write her own fictional stories. *Hood Symphony* is her first novel with a promise not to leave you hanging without a sequel.

G STREET CHRONICLES
~ PRESENTS ~

MONEY
IS THE ROOT
OF ALL EVIL

BOOSTERS

A NOVEL

SABRINA A. EUBANKS
AUTHOR OF *CHASING BLISS* & *FAME AND LOWLO* SHORT STORY SERIES

Quinn Whitaker is too smart for his own good. He and his close friends, Lonzo and Fitzi, have made a steady income out of shoplifting and petty thievery with Quinn masterminding their every move. The stakes change when they're presented with the opportunity to rob a drug dealer and increase their cash flow… but that move also changes the game. It whets Quinn's appetite to move on to the next big thing, and awakens his diabolical genius to master the craft and conquer the art of "the heist."

Lonzo and Fitzi come along for the ride of stealing big with Quinn as orchestrator, but when a simple job and blind luck leave them with more money than they ever dreamed of, the foundation of their friendship is eroded by greed, ego, distrust and murder. Quinn pushes past his aversion to taking lives and sets his sights on grabbing the brass ring – a job so big, so out of their league, it's unimaginable – but Quinn knows it can be done.

They say the love of money is the root of all evil. Will their friendship survive their quest to have it all, or will greed, envy, secrets and lust destroy them all?

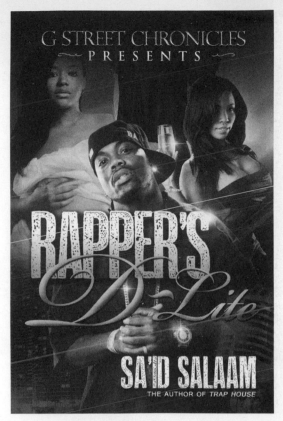

G STREET CHRONICLES
~ PRESENTS ~

RAPPER'S
D-Lite

SA'ID SALAAM
THE AUTHOR OF *TRAP HOUSE*

David Light, professionally known as D-Lite, wanted nothing else in life except to rap. His journey takes him from the mean streets of the South Bronx to the bright city lights of HotLanta!

Childhood friends, Desean and Shelby are along for the ride as faithful sidekicks. However, life at the top of the charts is more than they bargained for.

Success transforms David into the image created for him by his label. The lines between art and life blur as envy turns to jealousy and jealousy turns to murder.

Written by music business insider, Sa'id Salaam, Rapper's D-Lite is wildly entertaining but slyly intertwined with a moral message. In the end, decide for yourself if success is worth the price of fame.

The Love, Lies & Lust Series

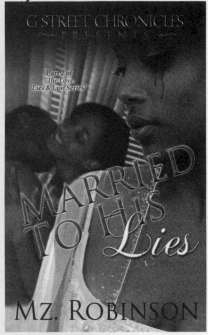

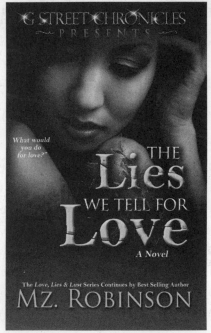

 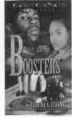   

We'd like to thank you for supporting G Street Chronicles and invite you to join our social networks. Please be sure to post a review when you're finished reading.

Facebook
G Street Chronicles
&
G Street Chronicles "A New Urban Dynasty" Readers' Group

Twitter
@gstrtchroni

My Space
G Street Chronicles

Email us and we'll add you to our mailing list
fans@gstreetchronicles.com

George Sherman Hudson, CEO
Shawna A. Grundy, VP